**PRESTON FICTION RESERVE**

CENTRAL LIBRARY
MARKET SQUARE
PRESTON: 53191

PP

THIS BOOK SHOULD ... THE LATEST
DATE SHOWN TO THE ... IT WAS BORROWED

- 0 JUN 1993    - 4 JUN 1994

23 JUL 1993

2 0 AUG 1993

- 5 NOV 1993

**AUTHOR**  EVANS, C.

**CLASS**  A F G

**TITLE**  Selected stories

Lancashire County Council
THE LANCASHIRE LIBRARY
Library Headquarters,
143, Corporation St.,
PRESTON PR1 2UQ
100% recycled paper

a30118 057275525b

# Selected Stories

Also by Caradoc Evans from Carcanet

*Nothing to Pay*

# CARADOC EVANS

### Selected Stories
Edited by John Harris

**CARCANET**

*Acknowledgements*

I am indebted to the following for permission to reproduce copyright material: the late Nicholas Sandys (literary executor), Seren Books (stories from *My People*), the Librarian, National Library of Wales (jacket photograph from the John Thomas collection); my thanks also to Simon Baker for discussing the content of this selection.

This selection first published in 1993 by
Carcanet Press Limited
208-212 Corn Exchange Buildings
Manchester M4 3BQ

Text copyright © 1993 The Estate of Caradoc Evans
Introduction and selection © 1993 John Harris
The right of John Harris to be identified
as the editor of this work has been asserted
by him in accordance with the Copyright,
Designs and Patents Act of 1988.
All rights reserved.

A CIP catalogue record for this book
is available from the British Library.
ISBN 0 85635 937 8

The publisher acknowledges financial assistance
from the Arts Council of Great Britain.

Set in 11pt Bembo by Bryan Williamson, Frome, Somerset
Printed and bound in England by SRP Ltd, Exeter

# Contents

'Our Antagonist is our Helper':
an introduction by John Harris   7

A Father in Sion   19
The Way of the Earth   27
Greater than Love   36
Be This Her Memorial   42
The Tree of Knowledge   47
The Pillars of Sion   54
The Deliverer   62
Judges   70
The Day of Judgment   74
The Acts of Dan   80
The Word   88
The Comforter   93
An Offender in Sion   100
A Widow Woman   105
Joseph's House   110
Earthbred   117
According to the Pattern   124
For Better   136
Saint David and the Prophets   143
Your Sin Will Find You Out   152
Changeable as a Woman with Child   159
A Widow with a Full Purse   167
Horse Hysbys and Oldest Brother   175
The Earth Gives All and Takes All   181

Bibliographical Notes   191

# 'Our Antagonist is our Helper': an introduction

These stories are mostly drawn from the five collections published by Caradoc Evans (1878-1945), three at the beginning and two towards the close of a writing career marked at either end by world war. His whole life as author was one continuous battle, with books suppressed, a play howled down in the West End, a radio talk banned by the BBC, his portrait on public display knife-slashed across the throat. As Evans remarked of his multitude of Christian critics, 'they are agreed that in a nicely conducted community I would, a handkerchief drawn over my eyes, have been placed against a blank wall long ago.' *My People* (1915) probed the rank underside of rural Wales: the greed and brutality, the patriarchal repression and chapel terrorism beneath the veneer of Nonconformist pronouncement. It was disturbingly original material from a Fleet Street journalist who had arrived in London as a draper's assistant, having toiled in shops since the age of fourteen. His schooling curtailed, he had been forced to leave home, the south Cardiganshire village where his widowed mother worked a nine-acre smallholding.

The years of counter slavery were years of mental awakening; in turn-of-the-century Cardiff and London Evans defined himself politically and began to discover literature in English:

the Continental writers (Zola, Maupassant, Chekhov, Tolstoy), the disciplined rage of Synge, Gissing on dehumanizing poverty, the London of Walter Besant and, above all, Charles Dickens. Devouring Forster's biography on leave from Whiteley's store, aspects of Dickens's background must have struck home: the family's sinking fortunes, indifference from those who could have helped, the agonies of menial employment – there was even a detested minister and an ignorant, tyrannical schoolmaster. Evans too resolved to escape further humiliation, moving into popular journalism following night classes in English at the Workingmen's College. From this period (1904–07) dates some apprentice work, 'tales of the mean streets' in the manner of Arthur Morrison and W.W. Jacobs. Though admiring their exploration of new fictional terrain, Evans came to accept that the world of the East End poor could never be his. 'The enemy of the novelist is the other novelist': his Cockney posing set aside, years elapsed before he discovered his own imaginative universe and the appropriate voice to describe it.

The creative release can be explained in terms of inner, emotional pressure, and a confidence and conviction strengthened by external circumstances (the year is 1914). 'I like stories that are gloomy morose and bitter, for I feel the author is chronicling the horrid sins of his enemies. An angry man is nearer himself than a happy man.' Passionate anger can provide artistic motive and, the venom controlled, produce explosive prose. For years Evans had been pondering his childhood in Rhydlewis and gathering incidents of life in the neighbourhood: savage, highly personal stories which seemed to confirm that the worse things done to Welshmen were done by other Welshmen, mostly in the name of religion. In Wales, as elsewhere, conditions of war deepened the social divide as already-dominant farmers displayed sinister new powers, manning the military tribunals and threatening to release for service farm-labourers bold enough to question wages or join a union. The big farmers, regularly the chapel elders, increased in prosperity also; 'in all wars the idealist fights for an imagined golden land, while the practical man gathers a golden harvest at home.' Behind the inequalities Evans discerned an abiding moral deformity, symptom of decayed religion, now a mix of anthropomorphism, superstition and the cruel self-righteousness of the Elect. Institutionalized religion had become the most potent repressive force, instilling mental obedience and legitimizing injustice. 'The modern saint expounds his gospel of love and sacrifice at the banquet table and he is at his best in a prayer meeting of millionaires.' Theocratic Wales, whose ministers walked with God and served the strong in the community, focused a condition of the times, while the Great War, far from shattering any meliorist illusions, bolstered Evans's conviction that strife was a natural state, that the injustices of the world are part of the world.

> We shall never have universal peace. At what time we shall not be fighting against a foreign enemy, we shall be fighting against our brothers and neighbours. Men will not cease to covet that which is not theirs, howsoever loudly they will cry forth their honesty. The humble shall serve the boastful; the rich shall be as gods, and they shall do no wrong, for the laws will be in their keeping.

The dark philosophy finds compelling expression in *My People* and *Capel Sion* (1916). Money worship, endemic brutality, the family as seat of violence, the debasement of women, class-bound religion as an index of standing and means of social control ('shed God and you shed nothing; shed respectability and you shed all'), these were not the qualities associated with rural Wales, a landscape known, if at all, through the sky-blue optimism of an Allen Raine. Equally arresting was Evans's linguistic medium, alien and authentic, an amalgam of biblical phrasing, translation from the Welsh (or aggressive mistranslation), and distorted English syntax. 'In the rendering of idiom you must create atmosphere. If the Bible or Tolstoy were done into straight English none of us would get nearer the life and conditions with which these authors deal.' To realize his world in 'straight English' was impossible; new content meant new expression and this bold refashioning of language came more readily to a native Welsh speaker. 'Foreigners write good English because they do not know English', Evans jotted in his notebook; the language could be approached free of in-built notions of propriety.

English critics welcomed the stories for their formal mastery ('not a single comment or superfluous word mars their tense directness') and hauntingly personal style. Evans was *sui generis* ('we know of nothing to put beside these merciless, sardonic silhouettes') though comparisons were invoked with Continental realism (Gorky, Zola, Maupassant on the Normandy peasantry) or English moral satire. Some right instinct had led to the Old Testament as a basis of style; perhaps (we might surmise) the only choice for a writer who from childhood had absorbed its rhythms. Welsh ministers may have suppressed folklore and fiction but the literary Bible survived to give Caradoc Evans his characteristic perspective, one that admits little external moralizing into the narrative. 'A novelist should neither praise nor blame. That's the preacher's job. His job is to tell the story.' And biblical cadence sharpens the satire: Evans impersonates what he wishes to condemn. Revealingly, his publisher Andrew Melrose attached the stories to a species of *Celtic* realism, that of conscious counterblast to romantic writing about homeland, exemplified by *The House with the Green Shutters*, George Douglas Brown's response to the tender pieties of the Scottish Kailyard tradition. We know that Evans admired Synge and the satirical Barrie, and that *Everyman*, when reviewing *A Portrait of the Artist as a Young Man*, dubbed Joyce the Irish Caradoc Evans ('astonishingly powerful and extraordinarily dirty'). In a Welsh context it was in contradistinction to Allen Raine that he first explained himself:

> Welsh novelists have in the past written stories which would have applied equally well to any part of the world if the geographical names had been altered. I myself wish to interpret the national life from within, to hold the mirror up to my countrymen and by displaying their weaknesses do

something to stimulate the great revitalisation for which all patriotic Welshmen are looking.

And this remained his defence: he was a reforming satirist, a patriot in his own terms if in no one else's.

From his compatriots came massive rejection: 'the literature of the sewer', 'a farrago of filth and debased verbal coinage'. In passionate rejoinders Evans spelt out the poisoned gifts of Calvinism.

> Nonconformity – a body without imagination and vision, a body which breaks down beliefs and traditions and all lovely things, and builds in their places hard materialism and avarice and hatred... I am still waiting for evidence of modern Welsh literature, of folklore, of spiritual vision, of drama and art. And I shall have to wait, because the stamina of my people has been robbed by a creed.

Rural Wales was a place of buried history and lost politics, the only dissension rising from wayward rebels (quietly bought over) or victimized women fighting not to go down. For those trapped in its compounds, 'the pillar of Nonconformity raised between them and Him', Evans saw no hope. 'As they were born; so will they live. They are the victims of a base religion. They have been whipped into something more destructive than unbelief.' A perfect précis of his fictional world. As for those hysterical attacks upon him,

> The leaders of Welsh nonconformity are uneasy that word of their tyranny will get into England. They and their members of Parliament have lied to the English how the heart of rural Wales is very beautiful, the pastors are fathers in Sion, and the peasants have neither spot nor blemish.

His analysis hits the mark. Idealization of the countryside reached the core of national identity, a mythology developing that in rural regions, not in the secularized industrial south, lay the true Wales, free of class conflict, social evil and religious doubt. Welsh political leaders furthered the notion of *heimat*, and there were signs that even the English were awakening to a Welshman's particular worth – which is why those of his countrymen brave enough to concede that Caradoc had a point still condemned him for sounding off outside the family and in an international language. The reality of Wales could never be known; what mattered was its projection in a widely circulating work of fiction (parallels with *The Satanic Verses* come to mind). Thus the ferocity of American Welsh reaction, after praise from reviewers like H.L. Mencken who saw laid bare in Caradoc Evans the fundamentalist habits of the American South; there too barbarism and booming piety went hand in hand (Mencken offered a hundred copies of *Capel Sion* to the YMCA).

*My Neighbours* (1920) turns its gaze upon the London Welsh, national exemplars like Ben Lloyd, a preacher-politician thriving in the commercial kingdom. Satire needs specific targets and behind Ben lies David Lloyd George, apotheosis of nationhood and faith. 'Mr George *is* Welsh nonconformity', agreed Evans, convinced of the presence seeking to suppress him. With an insider's knowledge (he was now subbing on the *Daily Mirror*) Evans mounted his attack: the Prime Minister was a sham, at once manipulator and puppet, advancing through cunning, flattery and mesmerizing rhetoric. His early radicalism discarded, Ben becomes the bosses' man, promising a servile labour force tamed by religious education. The key to his make-up is the community that bred him, its ingrained patriarchalism chillingly caught in a single sentence: from his marriage Ben's father receives much wealth and seven daughters, yet 'Even if Abel had land, money, and honour, his vessel of contentment was not filled until his wife went into her deathbed and gave him a son.' Interestingly the Ben Lloyd stories, though they vibrate with political animus, still do not encourage us to label Caradoc Evans a socialist or even a working-class writer. A palpable regard for the poor is never allowed to deflect his vision; he can summon up no heroes from amongst them nor convey any sense of their final victory. As they are born so must they live, rich and poor alike; all have sinned and fallen short of the glory. 'The trouble with our self-made god is that he is no stand-by in sorrow or affliction. In waste and weakness call we upon him never so hard, he is deaf and helpless and at the end we are alone and godless.' Thus 'According to the Pattern' ends with Ben's psychological disintegration; the godless life, the life of moral vacuity, is ultimately unsustainable.

Ben, as it happens, occasions a rich vein of comedy, as do Caradoc's ministers, in their matey parlance with the Almighty and perpetual scheming. In a world of petty pilferers the master rogues excite, and this author feeds off their inventiveness. Ben even talks his way out of hell, bypassing the divine rigmarole for measuring individual worth. For some the humour is of a kind removed from satire, the targets hero-villains beyond praise or blame; 'though it is not desirable' wrote the *TLS*, 'that every realist should be solemn, every performer in literature has to be serious, in the sense that he has to state events as he sees them; and this Mr Evans does.' The label 'realist' (and for that matter 'satirist') is rarely comfortable when applied to Caradoc Evans, though he discussed his work almost exclusively in terms of its 'realism'; Evans invests his writing with a drama and pathos not usually associated with satire, and if realism implies a breadth and balance of treatment he was never a realist. 'Magical realism' as well describes *My Neighbours*'s blend of eschatological fantasy and psychological truth: in the body of a returning soldier the Welsh patron saint gathers up the words of praying elders, floating in a chapel loft like pieces of a child's jig-saw puzzle. St David weaves a sack of cobwebs for his people's protestations. 'Jealous that no mishap should befall his treasure, he mounted a low, slow-moving cloud, and folding his wings rode up to the Gate of the Highway.' From the outset Evans moved confidently beyond naturalism and harnessed various comic modes: teasing irony, religious burlesque, violence and humour juxtaposed, black comedy of the grotesque.

'Joseph's House' proved a landmark story, with some favoured ingredients – the wronged widow, a canting minister sterner than his god – and a rarely admitted tenderness between mother and son worked with the conviction of Evans at his best ('the beautiful clear-cut simplicity of the story... is a joy', wrote Rhys Davies on rereading it). An autobiographical element intensifies the emotion and for the first time Evans explores his drapery background, the gentile refuge for sickly lads that proves their death trap. The abuse of shop assistants, their codes of survival, physical decay mirroring spiritual regression, these are elements foreshadowing *Nothing to Pay*, Evans's fine first novel, a Swiftian fable charting the progress of its miserly anti-hero through the drapery underworld at the turn of the century. Published in 1930, the book broke a long silence. The 1920s had been fallow years for Evans the writer though he prospered professionally, moving into literary journalism as acting editor of *T.P.'s Weekly*, the middle-brow periodical that also employed the Irish poet Austin Clarke. *Nothing to Pay* achieved some success, both critically and commercially, and buoyed by its reception Evans left London with the popular novelist Countess Barcynska ('Oliver Sandys') so as to devote himself to writing. Three disappointing novels were the rapid outcome, and for eight years he published nothing.

The return, when it came, was through the short story outwardly transformed. *Pilgrims in a Foreign Land* (1942) incorporates elements of folktale and the supernatural into a consciously more poetic medium, though its fantasy world is buttressed by the same grim truths of conflict and survival. Caradoc's men, dominant economically, remain 'talkists', lost in language and prey to obsession, unwilling to recognize what stares them in the face. The women, still social victims, are altogether more potent as individuals; emotionally alive, pragmatic and intuitive, they occupy every dimension, the sexual in particular. Now the often bloody victories are theirs: Pilgrim beheaded (the manner suggestive of castration), Katrin gaining her child and husbandless farm, and Miss Fach her disreputable pigger ('Cash is never dirty' the unspoken precept).

Only with the posthumously published *The Earth Gives All And Takes All* (1946) is the vision tempered. 'Two things are a farmer's delight, a horse who is glad to see him and a piecess of clay to warm', goals achieved (though not in that order) in 'Horse Hysbys and Oldest Brother' where Bensha, wife and horse contentedly work their mountain acres. In a caravan nearby lives Bensha's mother, whose protecting love has not always encompassed another woman. Seemingly there can be reconciliation on a Welsh hillside farm. In the title story, set on the eve of 'War Number Two', Evans approaches classic terrain with undiminished verve.

> Silah schoolen was a tidy bundle and she was dressed as if every day was a Sunday. She was not tall or short, fat or thin; her cheek-bones were high and her lips were wide and her top teeth swelled from her mouth in a showy white arch.
> The farmer came to the threshold of schoolhouse.
> 'Hoi-hoi,' he said. 'Stop the learning and come you here.'
> Silah came to him.
> 'Hear I do you are for auction,' he said.
> 'Who is the bidder?' asked Silah, pretending she did not know.
> 'A farmwr well to do.'
> 'What is the bid of the farmwr well to do?'
> 'Forty acres and livestock, dresser and coffer and press and settle and tables and chairs.'
> 'A man with no bed needs no wife.'
> 'Forget I did. A bed there is.'

Again a story of partners, in marriage and work, manoeuvring for advantage but with an ending which implies that men and women may come together, if along different paths. Like chapel mouthings the farmer's wisdom turns to dry dust in a loft; Ianto meanwhile is a pillar of good earth, 'and Silah and Ianto caressed and kneaded the earth and they poured their water upon its backward places'. The last antiphonal exchange, set in a stable, the talk moving around marriage and birth, fuses the human and natural worlds with the religious in a manner unexpected of Caradoc Evans.

Austin Clarke thought the later stories profoundly original achievements, proverbial in intensity and veined with 'a wild, harsh, unlovely poetry'. Good though they are, the blurring of narrative suggests an author less at ease in his intentions. Evans, we feel, is best on the attack, pressing the truth of his experience.

> We can only record a little of what we see and hear. The lie of today is the truth of tomorrow. Thus the novelist should convince himself that his story is true before he begins to write it; in that manner he will be able to tell his story as if he were telling the truth.

He excites as a courageously dissident force, refusing (as Raymond Williams notes of 'Anglo-Welsh' fiction writers in general) to leave to politicians, sociologists and historians the urgent social questions. (And the lie of yesterday is indeed the truth of today, an authority on the Welsh rural poor commenting that we might now accuse Evans not so much of malice as of understating his case!) He excites above all as a supreme storyteller: stories whose meaning lies in action, itself deriving from characters vividly before us as persons and types, embodied in the grain of their speech. The scrupulous functioning of narrative and dialogue Evans provocatively allied to journalism, not the literary kind ('solemn and ponderous and sonorous, counting style greater than matter') but that pursued in the dailies. 'They miss no points and waste no words', as he told an audience of apprentice writers. And clarity, simplicity and directness were the virtues of other exemplars, the Bible and *The Pilgrim's Progress*, 'the only two books that will help one to write – especially to write fiction.'

His first reader, Andrew Melrose, asked Caradoc whether Welsh life contained nothing more beautiful than was revealed in his stories. 'Oh yes,' he replied, 'but it is the ugly side of Welsh peasant life that I know most about.' That must be the answer to talk of Evans's narrowness of vision. He paints his picture as he sees it and in a manner wholly his own, a world of lapsed humanity where greed, lust and hypocrisy hold sway. What matters is not the nature of the vision but his power to express it. 'Why find fault because I write in the most engaging way I know? Is the builder blamed because he builds well?'

JOHN HARRIS

# A Father in Sion

On the banks of Avon Bern there lived a man who was a Father in Sion. His name was Sadrach, and the name of the farmhouse in which he dwelt was Danyrefail. He was a man whose thoughts were continually employed upon sacred subjects. He began the day and ended the day with the words of a chapter from the Book and a prayer on his lips. The Sabbath he observed from first to last; he neither laboured himself nor allowed any in his household to labour. If in the Seiet, the solemn, soul-searching assembly that gathers in Capel Sion on the nights of Wednesdays after Communion Sundays, he was entreated to deliver a message to the congregation, he often prefaced his remarks with, 'Dear people, on my way to Sion I asked God what He meant –'.

This episode in the life of Sadrach Danyrefail covers a long period; it has its beginning on a March night with Sadrach closing the Bible and giving utterance to these words:

'May the blessing of the Big Man be upon the reading of His Word.' Then, 'Let us us pray.'

Sadrach fell on his knees, the open palms of his hands together, his elbows resting on the table; his eight children – Sadrach the Small, Esau, Simon, Rachel, Sarah, Daniel, Samuel, and Miriam – followed his example.

Usually Sadrach prayed fluently, in phrases not unworthy of the minister, so universal, so intimate his pleading: tonight he stumbled and halted, and the working of his spiritful mind lacked the heavenly symmetry of the mind of the godly; usually the note of abundant faith and childlike resignation rang grandly throughout his supplications: tonight the note was one of despair and gloom. With Job he compared himself, for was not the Lord trying His servant to the uttermost? Would the all-powerful Big Man, the Big Man who delivered the Children of Israel from the hold of the Egyptians, give him a morsel of strength to bear his cross? Sadrach reminded God of his loneliness. Man was born to be mated, even as the animals in the fields. Without mate man was like an estate without an overseer, or a field of ripe corn rotting for the reaping-hook.

Sadrach rose from his knees. Sadrach the Small lit the lantern which was to light him and Esau to their bed over the stable.

'My children,' said Sadrach, 'do you gather round me now, for have I not something to tell you?'

Rachel, the eldest daughter, a girl of twelve, with reddish cheeks and bright eyes, interposed with:

'Indeed, indeed, now, little father; you are not going to preach to us this time of night!'

Sadrach stretched forth his hand and motioned his children be seated.

'Put out your lantern, Sadrach the Small,' he said. 'No, Rachel, don't you light the candle. Dear ones, it is not the light of this earth we need, but the light that comes from above.'

'Iss, iss,' Sadrach the Small said. 'The true light. The light the Big Man puts in the hearts of those who believe, dear me.'

'Well spoken, Sadrach the Small. Now be you all silent awhile, for I have things of great import to tell you. Heard you all my prayer?'

'Iss, iss,' said Sadrach the Small.

'Sadrach the Small only answers. My children, heard you all my prayer? Don't you be blockheads now – speak out.'

'There's lovely it was,' said Sadrach the Small.

'My children?' said Sadrach.

'Iss, iss,' they answered.

'Well, well, then. How can I tell you?' Sadrach put his fingers through the thin beard which covered the opening of his waistcoat, closed his eyes, and murmured a prayer. 'Your mother Achsah is not what she should be. Indeed to goodness, now, what disgrace this is! Is it not breaking my heart? You did hear how I said to the nice Big Man that I was like Job? Achsah is mad.'

Rachel sobbed.

'Weep you not, Rachel. It is not for us to question the all-wise ways of the Big Man. Do you dry your eyes on your apron now, my daughter. You, too, have your mother's eyes. Let me weep in my solitude. Oh, what sin have I committed, that God should visit this affliction on me?'

Rachel went to the foot of the stairs.

'Mam!' she called.

'She will not hear you,' Sadrach interrupted. 'Dear me, have I not put her in the harness loft? It is not respectable to let her out. Twm Tybach would have sent his wife to the madhouse of Carmarthen. But that is not Christian. Rachel, Rachel, dry your eyes. It is not your fault that Achsah is mad. Nor do I blame Sadrach the Small, nor Esau, nor Simon, nor Sarah, nor Daniel, nor Samuel, nor Miriam. Goodly names have I given you all. Live you up to them. Still, my sons and daughters, are you not all responsible for Achsah's condition? With the birth of each of you she has got worse and worse. Childbearing has made her foolish. Yet it is un-Christian to blame you.'

Sadrach placed his head in his arms.

Sadrach the Small took the lantern and he and Esau departed for their bed over the stable; one by one the remaining six put off their clogs and crept up the narrow staircase to their beds.

Wherefore to her husband Achsah became as a cross, to her children as one forgotten, to everyone living in Manteg and in the several houses scattered on the banks of Avon Bern as Achsah the madwoman.

The next day Sadrach removed the harness to the room in

the dwelling-house in which slept the four youngest children; and he put a straw mattress and a straw pillow on the floor, and on the mattress he spread three sacks; and these were the furnishings of the loft where Achsah spent her time. The frame of the small window in the roof he nailed down, after fixing on the outside of it three solid bars of iron of uniform thickness; the trap-door he padlocked, and the key of the lock never left his possession. Achsah's food he himself carried to her twice a day, a procedure which until the coming of Martha some time later he did not entrust to other hands.

Once a week when the household was asleep he placed a ladder from the floor to the loft, and cried:

'Achsah, come you down now.'

Meekly the woman obeyed, and as her feet touched the last rung Sadrach threw a cow's halter over her shoulders, and drove her out into the fields for an airing.

Once, when the moon was full, the pair were met by Lloyd the Schoolin', and the sight caused Mishtir Lloyd to run like a frightened dog, telling one of the women of his household that Achsah, the madwoman, had eyes like a cow's.

At the time of her marriage Achsah was ten years older than her husband. She was rich, too: Danyrefail, with its stock of good cattle and a hundred acres of fair land, was her gift to the bridegroom. Six months after the wedding Sadrach the Small was born. Tongues wagged that the boy was a child of sin. Sadrach answered neither yea nor nay. He answered neither yea nor nay until the first Communion Sabbath, when he seized the bread and wine from Old Shemmi and walked to the Big Seat. He stood under the pulpit, the fringe of the minister's Bible-marker curling on the bald patch on his head.

'Dear people,' he proclaimed, the silver-plated wine cup in one hand, the bread plate in the other, 'it has been said to me that some of you think Sadrach the Small was born out of sin. You do not speak truly. Achsah, dear me, was frightened by the old bull. The bull I bought in the September fair. You, Shemmi, you know the animal. The red-and-white bull. Well, well, dear people, Achsah was shocked by him. She was running away from him, and as she crossed the threshold of Danyrefail, did she not give birth to Sadrach the Small? Do you believe me now, dear people. As the Lord liveth, this is the truth. Achsah, Achsah, stand you up now, and say you to the congregation if this is not right.'

Achsah, the babe suckling at her breast, rose and murmured:
'Sadrach speaks the truth.'

Sadrach ate of the bread and drank of the wine.

Three months after Achsah had been put in the loft Sadrach set out at daybreak on a journey to Aberystwyth. He returned late at night, and, behold, a strange woman sat beside him in the horse car; and the coming of this strange woman made life different in Danyrefail. Early in the day she was astir, bustling up the children, bidding them fetch the cows, assist with the milking, feed the pigs, or do whatever work was in season.

Rachel rebuked Sadrach, saying, 'Little father, why for cannot I manage the house for you? Indeed now, you have given to Martha the position that belongs to me, your eldest daughter.'

'What mean you, my dear child?' returned Sadrach. 'Cast you evil at your father? Turn you against him? Go you and read your Commandments.'

'People are whispering,' said Rachel. 'They do even say that you will not be among the First Men of the Big Seat.'

'Martha is a gift from the Big Man,' answered Sadrach. 'She has been sent to comfort me in my tribulation, and to mother you, my children.'

'Mother!'

'Tut, tut, Rachel,' said Sadrach, 'Martha is only a servant in my house.'

Rachel knew that Martha was more than a servant. Had not her transfer letter been accepted by Capel Sion, and did she not occupy Achsah's seat in the family pew? Did she not, when it was Sadrach's turn to keep the minister's month, herself on each of the four Saturdays take a basket laden with a chicken, two white-hearted cabbages, a peck of potatoes, a loaf of bread, and half a pound of butter to the chapel house of Capel Sion? Did she not drive with Sadrach to market and fair and barter for his butter and cheese and cattle and what not? Did she not tell Ellen the Weaver's Widow what cloth to weave for the garments of the children of Achsah?

These things Martha did; and Danyrefail prospered exceedingly: its possessions spread even to the other side of Avon Bern. Sadrach declared in the Seiet that the Lord was heaping blessings on the head of His servant. Of all who worshipped in Sion none was stronger than the male of Danyrefail; none more respected. The congregation elected him to the Big Seat. Sadrach was a tower of strength unto Sion.

But in the wake of his prosperity lay vexation. Rachel developed fits; while hoeing turnips in the twilight of an afternoon she shivered and fell, her head resting in the water ditch that is alongside the hedge. In the morning Sadrach came that way with a load of manure.

'Rachel fach,' he said, 'wake you up now. What will Martha say if you get ill?'

He passed on.

When he came back Rachel had not moved, and Sadrach drove away, without noticing the small pool of water which had gathered over the girl's head. Within an hour he came again, and said:

'Rachel, Rachel, wake you up. There's lazy you are.'

Rachel was silent. Death had come before the milking of the cows. Sadrach went to the end of the field and emptied his cart of the manure. Then he turned and cast Rachel's body into the cart, and covered it with a sack, and drove home, singing the hymn which begins:

> 'Safely, safely gather'd in,
> Far from sorrow, far from sin,
> No more childish griefs or fears,
> No more sadness, no more tears;
> For the life so young and fair
> Now hath passed from earthly care;

God Himself the soul will keep,
Giving His beloved – sleep.'

Esau was kicked by a horse, and was hurt to his death; six weeks later Simon gashed his thumb while slicing mangolds, and he died. Two years went by, by the end of which period Old Ianto, the gravedigger of Capel Sion, dug three more graves for the children of Sadrach and Achsah; and over these graves Sadrach and Martha lamented.

But Sadrach the Small brought gladness and cheer to Danyrefail with the announcement of his desire to wed Sara Ann, the daughter of Old Shemmi. Martha and Sadrach agreed to the union provided Old Shemmi gave to his daughter a stack of hay, a cow in calf, a heifer, a quantity of bedclothes, and four cheeses. Old Shemmi, on his part, demanded with Sadrach the Small ten sovereigns, a horse and a cart, and a bedstead.

The night before the wedding Sadrach drove Achsah into the fields, and he told her how the Big Man had looked with goodwill upon Sadrach the Small, and was giving him Sara Ann to wife.

What occurred in the loft over the cowshed before dawn crept in through the window with the iron bars I cannot tell you. God can. But the rising sun found Achsah crouching behind one of the hedges of the lane that brings you from Danyrefail to the tramping road, and there she stayed, her eyes peering through the foliage, until the procession came by: first Old Shemmi and Sadrach, with Sadrach the Small between them; then the minister of Capel Sion and his wife; then the men and the women of the congregation; and last came Martha and Sara Ann.

The party disappeared round the bend: Achsah remained.

'Goodness me,' she said to herself. 'There's a large mistake now. Indeed, indeed, mad am I.'

She hurried to the gateway, crossed the road and entered another field, through which she ran as hard as she could. She came to a hedge, and waited.

The procession was passing.

Sadrach and Sadrach the Small.

Achsah doubled a finger.

Among those who followed on the heels of the minister was Miriam.

Achsah doubled another finger.

The party moved out of sight: Achsah still waited.

'Sadrach the Small and Miriam!' she said, spreading out her doubled-up fingers. 'Two. Others? Esau. Simon. Rachel. Sarah. Daniel. Samuel. Dear me, where shall I say they are? Six. Six of my children. Mad, mad am I?'... She laughed. 'They are grown, and I didn't know them.'

Achsah waited the third time for the wedding procession. This time she scanned each face, but only in the faces of Sadrach the Small and Miriam did she recognize her own children. She threw herself on the grass. Esau and Simon and Rachel, and Sarah and Daniel and Samuel. She remembered the circumstances attending the birth of each... And she had been a good wife. Never once did she deny Sadrach his rights. So long as she lasted she was a woman to him.

'Sadrach the Small and Miriam,' she said.

She rose and went to the graveyard. She came to the earth under which are Essec and Shan, Sadrach's father and mother, and at a distance of the space of one grave from theirs were the graves of six of the children born of Sadrach and Achsah. She parted the hair that had fallen over her face, and traced with her fingers the letters which formed the names of each of her six children.

\* \* \* \* \*

As Sara Ann crossed the threshold of Danyrefail, and as she set her feet on the flagstone on which Sadrach the Small is said to have been born, the door of the parlour was opened and a lunatic embraced her.

# The Way of the Earth

Simon and Beca are waiting for Death. The ten acres of land over Penrhos – their peat-thatched cottage under the edge of the moor – grows wilder and weedier. For Simon and Beca can do nothing now. Often the mood comes on the broken, helpless old man to speak to his daughter of the only thing that troubles him.

'When the time comes, Sara Jane fach,' he says, 'don't you hire the old hearse. Go you down to Dai the son of Mali, and Isaac the Cobbler, and Dennis the larger servant of Dan, and Twm Tybach, and mouth you like this to them: "Jasto, now, my little father Simon has gone to wear the White Shirt in the Palace. Come you then and carry him on your shoulders nice into Sion."'

'Yea, Sara fach,' Beca says, 'and speak you to Lias the Carpenter that you will give no more than ten over twenty shillings for the coffin.'

Simon adds: 'If we perish together, make you one coffin serve.'

Neither Simon nor Beca has further use for life. Paralysis shattered the old man the day of Sara Jane's wedding; the right side of his face sags, and he is lame on both his feet. Beca is blind, and she gropes her way about. Worse than all, they stand without the gates of Capel Sion – the living sin of all the land: they were married after the birth of Sara Jane, and though in the years of their passion they were all that a man and woman can be to each other, they begat no children. But Sion, jealous that not even his errant sheep shall lie in the parish graveyard and swell in appearance those who have worshipped the fripperies of the heathen Church, will embrace them in Death.

The land attached to Penrhos was changed from sterile moorland into a fertile garden by Simon and Beca. Great toil went to the taming of these ten acres of heather into the most fruitful soil in the district. Sometimes now Simon drags himself out into the open and complains when he sees his garden; and he calls Beca to look how the fields are going back to heatherland. And Beca will rise from her chair and feel her way past the bed which stands against the wooden partition, and as she touches with her right hand the ashen post that holds up the forehead of the house she knows she is facing the fields, and she too will groan, for her strength and pride are mixed with the soil.

'Sober serious, little Simon,' she says, 'this is the way of the earth, man bach.'

But she means that it is the way of mortal flesh... of her daughter Sara Jane, who will no longer give the land the labour it requires to keep it clean and good. Sara Jane has more than she can do in tending to her five-year-old twins and her dying parents, and she lets the fields pass back into wild moorland.

In the days of his sin and might Simon had been the useful man of Manteg. He was careless then that the gates of Sion were closed against him. He possessed himself of a cart and horse, and became the carrier between the cartless folk of Manteg and the townspeople of Castellybryn, eight miles down the valley. He and Beca saved; oil lamp nor candle never lit up their house, and they did not spend money on coal because peat was to be lifted just beyond their threshold. They stinted themselves in halfpennies, gathered the pennies till they amounted to shillings, put the silver in a box till they had five sovereigns' worth of it, and this sum Simon took to the bank in Castellybryn on his next carrier's journey. They looked to the time their riches would triumph over even Sion and so open for them the gates of the temple.

As soon as the Schoolin' allowed her to leave the Board School, Sara Jane was made to help Beca in all the farm work, thus enabling Simon to devote himself almost entirely to his neighbours. The man was covetous, and there were murmurings that strange sheaves of wheat were threshed on his floor, that his pigs fattened on other people's meal.

In accordance with the manner of labouring women Sara Jane wore clogs which had iron rims beneath them, grey stockings of coarse wool that were patched on the heels and legs with artless darns, and short petticoats; in all seasons her hands were chapped and ugly. Still with her auburn hair, her firm breast, and her white teeth, she was the desire of many. Farm servants ogled her in public places; farmers' sons lay in wait for her in lonely places. Men spoke to her frankly, and with counterfeit smiles in their faces; Sara Jane answered their lustful sayings with lewd laughter, and when the attack became too pressing she picked up her petticoats and ran home. Nor was she put out over the attentions she received: she was well favoured and she liked to be desired; and in the twilight of an evening her full-bosomed, ripe beauty struck Simon suddenly as he met her in the close. Her eyes were dancing with delight, and her breast heaving. Sadrach the Small had chased her right to Penrhos.

Simon and Beca discussed this that had happened, and became exceedingly afraid for her.

'There's an old boy, dear me, for you indeed!' said Simon. 'The wench fach is four over twenty now, and fretful I feel.'

'Iss, iss, Simon,' said Beca.

'If she was wedded now, she would be out of harm.'

'Wisdom you mouth, Simon. Good, serious me, to get her a male.'

'How say you then about Josi Cwmtwrch?'

'Clap your old lips, little man. Josi Cwmtwrch! What has Josi to give her? What for you talk about Josi?'

'Well, well, then. Tidy wench she is, whatever. And when we go she'll have the nice little yellow sovereigns in the bank.'

Beca interrupted: 'The eggs fetched three and ten pennies. Another florin now, Simon, and we've got five yellow sovereigns.'

'Don't say then! Pity that is. Am I not taking the old Schoolin's pig to Castellybryn on Friday too? Went you to all the old nests, woman fach?'

'Iss, man.'

'What is old Rhys giving for eggs now?'

'Five pennies for six. Big is the fortune the cheater is making.'

Beca dropped off her outer petticoat and drew a shawl over her head, and she got into bed; an hour later she was followed by Simon. In the morning she took to Shop Rhys three shillings' worth of eggs.

This was the slack period between harvests, and Sara Jane went with Simon to Castellybryn; and while Simon was weighing the Schoolin's pig she wandered hither and thither, and going over the bridge which spans Avon Teify she paused at the window of Jenkins Shop General, attracted thereto by the soaps and perfumes that were displayed.

'How are you?' said a young man at her side.

'Man bach, what for you fright me?' said Sara Jane. She was moved to step away, for she had heard read that the corners of streets are places of great temptation. The young man – a choice young man and comely: he wore spectacles, had the front of his hair trimmed in waves, and his moustaches ended in thin points – the young man seized her arm.

'Free you are, boy bach,' Sara Jane cried. 'Go you on now!'

'Come you in and take a small peep at my shop,' said the young man...

When Sara entered her father's cart she had hidden in the big pocket of her under-petticoat a cake of scented soap and a bottle of perfume.

That night she extracted the hobnails out of the soles of her Sabbath boots. That night also she collected the eggs, and for every three she gathered she concealed one. This she did for two more days, and the third day she purchased a blouse in

Shop Rhys. For this wastefulness her parents' wrath was kindled against her. The next Sunday she secretly used scented soap on her face and hands and poured perfume on her garments; and towards evening she traversed to the gateway where the moorland road breaks into the tramping way which takes you to Morfa-on-the-Sea. William Jenkins was waiting for her, his bicycle against the hedge; he was cutting the letters of his name into the gatepost. On the fourth night Sara Jane lay awake in bed. She heard the sound of gravel falling on the window pane, and she got up and let in the visitor.

The rumour began to be spread that William Jenkins, Shop General, was courting in bed with the wench of Penrhos, and it got to the ears of Simon and Beca.

'What for you want to court William Shinkins, Shop General, in bed for?' said Simon.

'There's bad you are,' said Beca.

'Is not Bertha Daviss saying that he comes up here on his old iron horse?' said Simon.

'Indeed to goodness,' answered Sara Jane, 'what is old Bertha doing out so late for? Say she to you that Rhys Shop was with her?'

'Speak you with sense, wench fach,' Beca said to her daughter.

'Is not William Shinkins going to wed me then?' said Sara Jane.

'Glad am I to hear that,' said Simon. 'Say you to the boy bach: "Come you to Penrhos on the Sabbath, little Shinkins."'

'Large gentleman is he,' said Sara Jane.

'Of course, dear me,' said Simon. 'But voice you like that to him.'

The Sabbath came, and people on their way to Capel Sion saw William Jenkins go up the narrow Roman road to Penrhos, and they said one to another: 'Close will be the bargaining.' Simon was glad that Sara Jane had found favour in William's eyes: here was a godly man and one of substance; he owned a Shop General, his coat was always dry, and he wore a collar every day in the week, and he received many red pennies in the course of a day. Simon took him out on the moor.

'Shall we talk this business then at once?' Mishtir Jenkins observed. 'Make plain Sara Jane's inheritance.'

'Much, little boy.'

'Penrhos will come to Sara Jane, then?'

'Iss, man.'

'Right that is, Simon. Wealthy am I. Do I not own Shop General? Man bach, there's a grand business for you!'

'Don't say!'

'Move your tongue now about Sara Jane's wedding portion,' said Mishtir Jenkins.

'Dear me, then, talk will I to Beca about this thing,' answered Simon.

Three months passed by. Sara Jane moaned because that her breast was hurtful. Beca brewed for her camomile tea, but the pains did not go away. Then at the end of a day Sara Jane told Beca and Simon how she had done.

'Concubine!' cried Beca.

'Harlot!' cried Simon.

'For sure me, disgrace this is,' said Beca.

Sara Jane straightened her shoulders.

'Samplers bach nice you are!' she said maliciously. 'Crafty goats you are. What did the old Schoolin' use to say when he called the names in the morning? "Sara Jane, the bastard of Simon and Beca." Iss, that's the old Schoolin'. But William Shinkins will wed me. I shan't be cut out of the Seiet.'

Simon and Beca were distressed.

'Go you down, little Simon, and word to the boy,' said Beca.

'I've nothing to go for,' replied Simon.

'Hap Madlen Tybach need coal?'

'No-no. Has she not much left? Did I not look upon the coal when I fetched the eggs?'

'Sorrowful it is you can find no errand. Wise would be to speech to the male bach.'

'Dear little me! I'll go round and ask the tailor if he is expecting parcels from the station.'

'Do you now. You won't be losing money if you can find a little errand.'

At dawn Simon rose and went to Castellybryn. In going over the bridge of Avon Teify he halted and closed his eyes and prayed. This is his prayer: 'Powerful Big Man bach, deal you fair by your little servant. And if Shinkins, Shop General, says, "I am not the father of your wench's child," strike him dead. We know he is. Ask you Bertha Daviss. Have we not seen his name on the gatepost? This, Jesus bach, in the name of the little White Jesus.'

Outside Shop General he called in a loud voice: 'William Shinkins, where he is?' Then he came down and walked into the parlour where Mishtir Jenkins was eating.

Simon said: 'Sara Jane is with child.'

'And say you do that to me,' said Mishtir Jenkins.

'Iss, iss, man. Sore is Beca about it.'

'Don't you worry, Simon bach, the time is long.'

'Mishtir Shinkins. There's religious he is,' said Simon, addressing William Jenkins in the third person, as is the custom in West Wales when you are before your betters. 'Put him up the banns now then.'

'I will, Simon.'

'Tell he me, when shall I say to Beca thus: "On such and such a day is the wedding"? Say him a month this day?'

'All right, Simon. I'll send the old fly from the Drovers' Arms to bring you and Sara Jane. Much style there will be. Did you voice to Beca about the matter?'

'What was that now, indeed, Mishtir Shinkins?'

'Why was you so dull? Sara Jane's portion, old boy.'

'Well-well, iss. Well-well, no. We're poor in Penrhos, Mishtir Shinkins. Poor.'

'Grudging you are with your money, Simon Penrhos.'

'Don't he say like that. Make speech will I again with Beca.'

Mishtir Jenkins stretched his face towards Simon, and said:

'What would you say, Simon, if I asked you to give me Sara Jane's portion this one small minute?'

'Waggish is his way, little Shinkins bach,' said Simon with pretended good humour.

'My father had a farm and sovereigns and a cow when he wedded.'

'Open my lips to Beca I will about this,' answered Simon.

'Good, very,' replied Mishtir Jenkins. 'I will say about the wedding, man, when you bring me Beca's words.'

'Shinkins! Shinkins!'

'Leave you me half a hundred of pounds of Sara Jane's portion and I'll stand by my agreement.'

'Joking he is, William Shinkins. Deal well we will by Sara Jane on the day of her wedding.'

William Shinkins spoke presently. 'I am not a man to go back on my promise to Sara Jane,' he said. 'And am I not one of respect?'

Simon went home and gave thanks unto God Who had imparted understanding to the heart of William Jenkins. But folks in Manteg declared that designing men crossed the river in search of females to wed. Sara Jane was no longer ashamed. She went about and abroad and wore daily the boots from which she had taken out the hobnails.

On the appointed day the fly came to Penrhos, and Simon and Sara Jane went away in it: and as they passed through Manteg Bertha Daviss cried: 'People bach, tell you me where you are going.'

Simon told her the glad news.

Bertha waved her hand, and she cried to the driver: 'Boy nice, whip up, whip up, or you'll have another passenger to carry.'

Mishtir Jenkins met Simon and Sara Jane at the door of the inn.

'Sara Jane,' he said, 'stop you outside while me and your father expound to each other.'

He took Simon into the stable.

'Did you ask Beca about the yellow sovereigns?' he said.

'Iss, iss. Many sovereigns he will get.'

'How many?'

'Shinkins bach, why for he hurry? Bad it looks.'

'Sound the figures now, Simon.'

'Ten yellow sovereigns, dear me.'

'Simon Penrhos, you and your wench go home.'

'William Shinkins, he knows that Sara Jane is full. I'll inform against him. The law of the Sessions I'll put on him. Indeed I will.'

'Am I not making Sara Jane mistress of Shop General? Solemn me, serious it is to wed a woman with child!'

'There's hard he is, Shinkins. Take two over ten sovereigns and a little parcel of potatoes, and a few white cabbages, and many carrots.'

'Is that your best offer, Simon?'

'It's all we have, little man. We're poor.'

'Go with the wench. Costly the old fly is for me.'

Simon seized Mishtir Jenkins' coat.

'William Shinkins bach,' he cried, 'don't he let his anger get the better of his goodness. Are we not poor? Accept he our daughter –'

'Simon Penrhos, one hundred of pounds you've got in the bank, man. Give me that one hundred this morning before the wedding. If you don't do that you shall see.'

Simon shivered. He was parting with his life. It was his life and Beca's life. She had made it, turning over the heather, and wringing it penny by penny from the stubborn earth. He, too, had helped her. He had served his neighbours, and thieved from them. He wept.

'He asks too much,' he cried. 'Too much.'

'Come, now, indeed,' said William Jenkins. 'Do you act religious by the wench fach.'

Simon went with him to the bank, and with a smudge and a cross blotted out his account. Then he witnessed the completion of the bargain in Capel Baptists, which is beyond the Sycamore Tree.

The bridegroom took the bride home to Shop General, and he gave half of the dowry to a broker's man who had been put in possession. Some of the remaining fifty sovereigns went to his landlord for overdue rent, and on the rest William Jenkins and Sara Jane lived for nearly a year. Then the broker's man returned, wherefore William Jenkins gave over the fight and fled out of the land.

## *Greater than Love*

Esther knew the sun had risen because she could number the ripening cheeses arrayed on the floor against the wall. She threw back the shawl and sacks that covered her, and descending by the ladder into the kitchen, withdrew the bolt and opened the door.

'Goodness all! Late terrible am I,' she said to the young man who entered. 'Bring you the cows in a hurry, boy bach.'

'Talk you like that, Esther, when the old animals are in the close.'

Esther knelt on the hearth and lit the dried furze thereon.

'The buckets are in the milk-house,' she went on. 'Boy bach, hie you away off and make a start. Come I will as soon as I am ready.'

The young man shuffled across the floor into the dairy. He came back with two buckets and a wooden tub, and he placed the tub on the ground and sat on its edge.

'This is the day of the seaside,' he said.

Esther turned her face away from the smoke that ascended from the fire.

'Indeed, indeed, now, Sam bach!' she cried, 'and you don't say so then!'

'Esther fach, vexful the move of your tongue. Say to me whose cart is carting you?'

'Who speeched that I was going, Sam the son of Ginni?'

'Don't you be laughing, Esther. Tell me now whose cart is carting you.'

'Go I would for sure into Morfa, but, dear me, no one will have me,' said Esther.

'What for you cry mischief when there's no mischief to be?' said Sam.

Esther tore off pieces of peat and arranged them lightly on the furze.

'Nice place is Morfa,' she observed.

'Girl fach, iss,' Sam said. 'Nice will be to go out in Twmmi's boat. Speak you that you will spend the day with me.'

'How say Catrin! Sober serious! How will Catrin the daughter of Rachel speak if you don't go with her?'

'Mention you Catrin, Esther fach, what for?'

'Is there not loud speakings that you have courted Catrin in bed? Very full is her belly.'

'Esther! Esther! Why you make me savage like an old rabbit? Why for play old pranks? Wench fach, others have been into Catrin. If I die, this is true. Do you believe me now?'

Esther plagued him, saying:

'Bring me small fairings home, Sam bach. Did I not give you a knife when I went to the Fair of the Month of April?'

Sam took out his knife, and sharpened the blade on the leather of his clog.

'Grateful was I for the nice knife,' he said. 'Did I not stick Old Shemmi's pig with it, Esther fach?'

'Well-well, then?'

'Look you, there's old murmuring that you were taken in mischief with the Schoolin' in Abram's hen loft,' said Sam.

Esther rose to her feet and looked upon him. This is the manner of man she saw: a short, bent-shouldered, stunted youth; his face had never been shaved and was covered with tawny hair, and his eyes were sluggish.

Esther laughed.

'Boy bach, unfamiliar you are,' she said.

'Mam did say,' Sam proceeded, 'that I ought not to wed a shiftless female who doesn't take Communion in Capel Sion.'

'Your mother Old Ginni is right,' said Esther. 'Keep you on with Catrin. Ugly is Catrin with bad pimples in her face. But listen you, Sam; a large ladi I will be. I don't want louts like you.'

The fire was under way; Esther rolled up to her waist her outer petticoat and she put on an apron.

'Why sit you there like a donkey?' she cried. 'Away you and do the milking.'

'Ester fach, come you to Morfa,' Sam pleaded.

'For sure I'm coming to Morfa,' Esther answered. 'But not with you. Am I not going to find a love there?'

Then they went forth into the close to milk Old Shemmi's cows, and while they did so each chanted:

> 'There's a nice cow is Gwen!
> Milk she gives indeed!
> More milk, little Gwen; more milk!
> A cow fach is Gwen,' –

thereby coaxing the animals to give their full yield.

When the milk was separated Esther put on her Sabbath garments and drew her red hair tightly over her forehead, and she took her place in Shemmi's hay waggon. There were many in the waggon other than Esther and Sam, for the custom is that the farmer takes his servants and those who have helped him without payment in the hayfield freely on a set day to the Sea of Morfa.

Shemmi's waggon reached Morfa before the dew had lifted, and towards the heat of the day (after they had eaten) the people of Manteg gathered together. One said: 'Come you down to the brim now, and let us wash our little bodies.' The men bathed nakedly: the women had brought spare petticoats with them, and these they wore when they were in the water.

Esther changed her behaviour when she got to Morfa, and she feigned herself above all who had come from Manteg, and while she sat alone in the shadow of a cliff there came to her Hws Morris, a young man who was in training to be a minister. Mishtir Morris was elegant: his clothes were black and he had a white collar round his neck and white cuffs at the ends of his sleeves, and on his feet he had brown shoes of canvas.

Hws Morris took off from his head his black hat, which was of straw, and said to Esther:

'Sure now, come you from Squire Pryce's household? You are his daughter indeed?'

'Stranger bach,' answered Esther, 'say you like that, what for?'

'A ladi you seem,' said Hws Morris.

Esther was vain, and she did not perceive through the man's artifice.

'Indeed, indeed, then,' said Hws Morris, 'speak from where you are.'

'Did you not say I was Squire Pryce's daughter?' said Esther.

'Ho, ho, old boy wise is Squire Pryce.'

Esther turned her eyes upon the bathers. Catrin and another woman were knee-deep in the water; between them, their hands linked, Sam. She heard Bertha Daviss crying from the shore: 'Don't you wet it, Sam bach.'

Hws Morris placed the tips of his fingers into his ears.

'This,' he mourned, 'after two thousand years of religion. They need the little Gospel.'

'Very respectable to be a preacher it is,' said Esther.

'And to be a preacher's mistress,' said Hws Morris. 'Great is the work the Big Man has called me to do.'

A murmuring came from the women on the beach: Sam was struggling in the water. Esther moved a little nearer the sea.

'Where was you going to, then?' asked Hws Morris. 'You was not going to bathe with them?'

'Why for no?'

'See you how immodest they are. Girl fach, stay you here. If you need to wash your body, go you round to the backhead of the old stones and take off your clothes and bathe where no eyes will gaze on you.'

The murmuring now sounded violent: Lloyd the Schoolin' was swimming towards Sam.

Esther passed beyond the stones, and in a cave she cast off her clothes and walked into the sea; and having cleansed herself, she dried her skin in the heat of the sun. When she got out from the cave, Hws Morris came up to her.

'Hungry you are,' he said to her. 'Return you into the cave and eat a little of this cake.'

He led her far inside, so far that they could not see anything that was outside. Hws Morris placed his arm over Esther's shoulders, and his white fingers moved lightly over her breast to her thigh. He stole her heart.

Esther heard a voice crying her name.

'Wench fach,' said Hws Morris to her, 'let none know of our business.'

Sam shouted her name against the rocks and over the sea; he cried it in the ears of strange people and at the doors of strange houses. Towards dusk he said to the women who were waiting for Shemmi's hay waggon to start home: 'Little females, why is Esther not here?'

Catrin jeered at him: 'Filling her belly is Esther.'

'But say you've seen Esther fach!' Sam cried.

'Twt, twt!' said Bertha Daviss. 'What's the matter with the boy? Take him in your arms, Catrin, and take him to your bed.'

'Speak you Esther is not drowned,' Sam urged.

'Drowned!' Catrin repeated loudly. 'Good if the bad concubine is.'

'Evil is the wench,' said Bertha Daviss. 'Remember how she tried to snare Rhys Shop.'

'Fond little women,' Sam cried, 'say you that Esther fach is not drowned.'

'Sam, indeed to goodness,' Bertha said to him, 'trouble not your mind about a harlot.'

'Now, dear me,' answered Sam, 'foolish is your speech, Bertha. How shall I come home without Esther?'

'There's Catrin, Sam bach. Owe you nothing to Catrin? Is she not in child by you?'

Old Shemmi's hay waggon came into the roadway, and Sam said to the man who drove the horse:

'Male bach nice, don't you begin before Esther comes, and she will be soon. Maybe she's sleeping.'

'In the arms of a man,' said Catrin.

Sam placed his hands around his mouth and shouted Esther's name.

The people entered the waggon: Sam remained in the road.

'Find you her, Sam bach!' Catrin cried. 'Ask the Bad Spirit if he has seen her.'

Old Shemmi's mare began the way home.

Sam hastened back to the beach: the tide was coming in, and he walked through the waters, shouting, moaning, and lamenting. At last he beheld Esther, and an awful wrath was kindled within him. As he had loved her, so he now hated her: he hated even more than he had loved her. He had gone on the highway that ends in Llanon. At a little distance in front of him he saw her with a man, and he crept close to them and he heard their voices. He heard Esther saying:

'Don't you send me away now. Let me stay with you.'

The man answered: 'Shut your throat, you temptress. For why did you flaunt your body before my religious eyes?'

'Did you not make fair speeches to me?' said Esther.

'Terrible is your sin,' said the man. 'Turn away from me. Little Big Man bach, forgive me for eating of the wench's fruit.'

Sam came up to them by stealth.

'Out of your head you must be, boy bach, to make sin with Esther,' he said.

Hws Morris looked into Sam's face, and a horrid fear struck him, and he ran: and Sam opened his knife and running after him, caught him and killed him. He had difficulty in drawing away the blade, because it had entered into the man's skull. Then he returned to the place where Esther was, and her he killed also.

## Be This Her Memorial

Mice and rats, as it is said, frequent neither churches nor poor men's homes. The story I have to tell you about Nanni – the Nanni who was hustled on her way to prayer-meeting by the Bad Man, who saw the phantom mourners bearing away Twm Tybach's coffin, who saw the Spirit Hounds and heard their moanings two days before Isaac Penparc took wing – the story I have to tell you contradicts that theory.

Nanni was religious; and she was old. No one knew how old she was, for she said that she remembered the birth of each person that gathered in Capel Sion; she was so old that her age had ceased to concern.

She lived in the mud-walled, straw-thatched cottage on the steep road which goes up from the Garden of Eden, and ends at the tramping way that takes you into Cardigan town; if you happen to be travelling that way you may still see the roofless walls which were silent witnesses to Nanni's great sacrifice – a sacrifice surely counted unto her for righteousness, though in her search for God she fell down and worshipped at the feet of a god.

Nanni's income was three shillings and ninepence a week. That sum was allowed her by Abel Shones, the officer for Poor Relief, who each pay-day never forgot to remind the crooked, wrinkled, toothless old woman how much she owed to him and God.

'If it was not for me, little Nanni,' Abel was in the habit of telling her, 'you would be in the House of the Poor long ago.'

At that remark Nanni would shiver and tremble.

'Dear heart,' she would say in the third person, for Abel was a mighty man and the holder of a proud office, 'I pray for him night and day.'

Nanni spoke the truth, for she did remember Abel in her prayers. But the workhouse held for her none of the terrors it holds for her poverty-stricken sisters. Life was life anywhere, in cottage or in poorhouse, though with this difference: her liberty in the poorhouse would be so curtailed that no more would she be able to listen to the spirit-laden eloquence of the Respected Josiah Bryn-Bevan. She helped to bring Josiah into the world; she swaddled him in her own flannel petticoat; she watched him going to and coming from school; she knitted for him four pairs of strong stockings to mark his going out into the world as a farm servant; and when the boy, having obeyed the command of the Big Man, was called to minister to the congregation of Capel Sion, even Josiah's mother was not more vain than Old Nanni. Hence Nanni struggled on less than three shillings and ninepence a week, for did she not give a tenth of her income to the treasury of the Capel? Unconsciously she came to regard Josiah as greater than God: God was abstract; Josiah was real.

As Josiah played a part in Nanni's life, so did a Seller of Bibles play a minor part in the last few days of her travail. The man came to Nanni's cottage the evening of the day of the rumour that the Respected Josiah Bryn-Bevan had received a call from a wealthy sister church in Aberystwyth. Broken with grief, Nanni, the first time for many years, bent her stiffened limbs and addressed herself to the living God.

'Dear little Big Man,' she prayed, 'let not your son bach religious depart.'

Then she recalled how good God had been to her, how He had permitted her to listen to His son's voice; and another fear struck her heart.

'Dear little Big Man,' she muttered between her blackened gums, 'do you now let me live to hear the boy's farewell words.'

At that moment the Seller of Bibles raised the latch of the door.

'The Big Man be with this household,' he said, placing his pack on Nanni's bed.

'Sit you down,' said Nanni, 'and rest yourself, for you must be weary.'

'Man,' replied the Seller of Bibles, 'is never weary of well-doing.'

Nanni dusted for him a chair.

'No, no; indeed now,' he said; 'I cannot tarry long, woman. Do you not know that I am the Big Man's messenger? Am I not honoured to take His word into the highways and byways, and has He not sent me here?'

He unstrapped his pack, and showed Nanni a gaudy volume with a clasp of brass, and containing many coloured prints; the pictures he explained at hazard: here was a tall-hatted John baptizing, here a Roman-featured Christ praying in the Garden of Gethsemane, here a frock-coated Moses and the Tablets.

'A Book,' said he, 'which ought to be on the table of every Christian home.'

'Truth you speak, little man,' remarked Nanni. 'What shall I say to you you are asking for it?'

'It has a price far above rubies,' answered the Seller of Bibles. He turned over the leaves and read: '"The labourer is worthy of his hire." Thus it is written. I will let you have one copy – one copy only – at cost price.'

'How good you are, dear me!' exclaimed Nanni.

'This I can do,' said the Seller of Bibles, 'because my Master is the Big Man.'

'Speak you now what the cost price is.'

'A little sovereign, that is all.'

'Dear, dear; the Word of the little Big Man for a sovereign!'

'Keep you the Book on your parlour table for a week. Maybe others who are thirsty will see it.'

Then the Seller of Bibles sang a prayer; and he departed.

Before the week was over the Respected Josiah Bryn-Bevan announced from his pulpit that in the call he had discerned the voice of God bidding him go forth into the vineyard.

Nanni went home and prayed to the merciful God:

'Dear little Big Man, spare me to listen to the farewell sermon of your saint.'

Nanni informed the Seller of Bibles that she would buy the Book, and she asked him to take it away with him and have written inside it an inscription to the effect that it was a gift from the least worthy of his flock to the Respected Josiah Bryn-Bevan, D.D., and she requested him to bring it back to her on the eve of the minster's farewell sermon.

She then hammered hobnails into the soles of her boots, so as to render them more durable for tramping to such capels as Bryn-Bevan happened to be preaching in. Her absences from home became a byword, occurring as they did in the haymaking season. Her labour was wanted in the fields. It was the property of the community, the community which paid her three shillings and ninepence a week.

One night Sadrach Danyrefail called at her cottage to commandeer her services for the next day. His crop had been on the ground for a fortnight, and now that there was a prospect of fair weather he was anxious to gather it in. Sadrach was going to say hard things to Nanni, but the appearance of the gleaming-eyed creature that drew back the bolts of the door frightened him and tied his tongue. He was glad that the old woman did not invite him inside, for from within there issued an abominable smell as might have come from the boiler of the witch who one time lived on the moor. In the morning he saw Nanni trudging towards a distant capel where the Respected Josiah Bryn-Bevan was delivering a sermon in the evening. She looked less bent and not so shrivelled up as she did the night before. Clearly, sleep had given her fresh vitality.

Two Sabbaths before the farewell sermon was to be preached Nanni came to Capel Sion with an ugly sore at the side of her mouth; repulsive matter oozed slowly from it, forming into a head, and then coursing thickly down her chin on to the shoulder of her black cape, where it glistened among the beads. On occasions her lips tightened, and she swished a hand angrily across her face.

'Old Nanni,' folk remarked while discussing her over their dinner-tables, 'is getting as dirty as an old sow.'

During the week two more sores appeared; the next Sabbath Nanni had a strip of calico drawn over her face.

Early on the eve of the farewell Sabbath the Seller of Bibles arrived with the Book, and Nanni gave him a sovereign in small money. She packed it up reverently, and betook herself to Sadrach Danyrefail to ask him to make the presentation.

At the end of his sermon the Respected Josiah Bryn-Bevan made reference to the giver of the Bible, and grieved that she was not in the Capel. He dwelt on her sacrifice. Here was a Book to be treasured, and he could think of no one who would treasure it better than Sadrach Danyrefail, to whom he would hand it in recognition of his work in the School of the Sabbath.

In the morning the Respected Josiah Bryn-Bevan, making a tour of his congregation, bethought himself of Nanni. The thought came to him on leaving Danyrefail, the distance betwixt which and Nanni's cottage is two fields. He opened the door and called out:

'Nanni.'

None answered.

He entered the room. Nanni was on the floor.

'Nanni, Nanni!' he said. 'Why for you do not reply to me? Am I not your shepherd?'

There was no movement from Nanni. Mishtir Bryn-Bevan went on his knees and peered at her. Her hands were clasped tightly together, as though guarding some great treasure. The minister raised himself and prised them apart with the ferrule of his walking-stick. A roasted rat revealed itself. Mishtir Bryn-Bevan stood for several moments spellbound and silent; and in the stillness the rats crept boldly out of their hiding places and resumed their attack on Nanni's face. The minister, startled and horrified, fled from the house of sacrifice.

# The Tree of Knowledge

Watkin Pensarn died, and his children were: Ben, Dennis, Mari. Ben inherited Pensarn and also the Field of the Tree – which is on the edge of the moor – and the mud-walled cottage therein. Mari did not receive anything, because of her whorish ways: she had had seven children by seven men. But Ben showed kindness unto her: he made her a servant on his land and he let her abide in the cottage which is in the Field of the Tree.

Dennis dwelt in Glasgoed, which is in the valley. He did not inherit anything. In the safety of his thirty-eight acres of land, a living house and outhouses, and one hundred and ten sovereigns, he offended against Sion. So the Big Man was angered and caused him to be persecuted and to commit the sin whose awfulness is above all other sins. The period of his infliction began when he rented the Field of the Tree from Ben and repaired the hedge around it and strewed manure on the floor of it, saying: 'A hayfield will I make of the place bach.' Before long he beheld that a narrow path was trodden down between the gate and Mari's house. His mind became stormy, and he shouted: 'Mari, now, indeed, where you was? Why for you mess my hay?'

Mari moved to him.

'Blasted you are, bad wench, in my small eyes,' Dennis cried. 'Full of frogs is your carrion.'

'This one moment, Dennis bach, windy you are,' Mari replied. 'Say you why to me.'

'What you walk upon my grass? See you that you spoil my hay! A nasty lizard, dear me, you was.'

'Vexed is your head,' Mari answered. 'Do you, Dennis Glasgoed, show me how to reach the road.'

Having abused his sister with these words: 'Speech like an old crow you do,' Dennis lifted the gate and the gate posts from the gap which was in the hedge and thereon he raised a wall of earth and stones, and into this new wall he cunningly contrived broken glass. Mari climbed over the hedge at another place and soon she made a deep opening in it. One night a cow came into the field and feasted. Dennis wept when he viewed the havoc the animal had made and spoke harshly to Mari; and as he spoke his rage was increased that there was another path between the house and the spring which yields fresh water.

'Sober serious,' said Mari, 'what does the man bach want? Weary am I of life. Do I not wish I was a hundred years ago?'

'Walk you away from here,' Dennis answered. 'Destroyer very terrible you are.'

Dennis measured the length and breadth of the pathways and he thought out the bulk of hay he had lost, and the bulk was as much as two persons can pitch twice from field into cart. That knowledge pained him, and he went up to Ben: 'Jasto, now, cheated me you have over the old field.'

'Boy bach Glasgoed,' said Ben. 'Mouth you like that, for sure. Open wider the back of your head.'

'The house in the field you give to Mari. There's a serpent in the shipsy.'

'Is not the Big Man's curse on Mari, Dennis? Does He not torment her breast with an ulcer?'

'No care have I for that,' cried Dennis. 'Messed my hay bach she has. Nice grass there was in the paths.'

'Well, you don't mean.'

'Look you, iss – iss. But loutish you are. Shake yourself in my favour.'

'Come you into the parlour bach,' said Ben, 'and I will hold forth.' Therein Ben spat upon the floor and knelt. This is what he told God: 'A black of a donkey was Cain. Brothers we all are, little Big Man. Dennis Glasgoed is here. Solemn is the thing that has happened to his hay. Be with your son in Sion. Amen.' Before he arose he opened his eyes and he placed a finger and a thumb above his hairy nostrils and blew the residue therefrom upon the floor. Presently he charged the cast of his face with grief; and he spoke: 'Certain, Dennis Glasgoed. Cheapish is the little field.'

Dennis understood: 'A cunning herring you are.'

'Speak you do like that. Well – well.'

'Well – well?'

'Pay you me one sovereign and a half a sovereign every year and Mari's house you shall have,' said Ben.

'Big Father, no – no! Poor am I.'

'Losing very great am I to give you the house. But are you not my brother?'

'Half a yellow sovereign, Ben bach nice. Not worth killing is the hay. Cart a load of coals I will, too.'

'No, man. Farewell, now.'

Dennis rented Mari's house for fifteen shillings and a load of fairly turned dung, wherefore he devised a lying scheme; he said to Mari: 'Stir off. Savage is the bull that I put in your house.'

'Stir will I,' replied Mari, 'the minute I hear the noise of his coming.'

When Dennis was returned to Glasgoed his wife Madlen was perturbed and in much fear. 'Horrible is this. Guiltless am I.'

'What is the matter with the strollop? Be you hasty,' said Dennis.

'Perished is the ass fach.'

Dennis did not chasten his wife. 'Where is the carcase?'

'Sure me,' Madlen answered, 'boiling is the head for the pigs.'

"Fool of a squirrel! Do you that, for why? Talk where the ass is.'

'In the milk house is the body bach, covered with my petticoat.'

Dennis put the ass in a sack which had held white flour and which was whitened therewith, and the next night he took the ass and also a pickaxe and a shovel to the Field of the Tree. He dug a hole in the ground and when he reached the water which flows into the spring, he hung the sack on the Tree and put the ass in the hole. As he was coming away, he said to himself: 'Turks are persons, and robbers. Ben will take from me all that I have. Mari pilfers two pitches of my hay.'

He walked down straightway into the Tramping road, and on all sides and around him he heard noises; he lifted his eyes and saw birds passing between him and the moon. He crawled over the last hedge into the road, and his gaze fell upon a shadow moving on the face of it. He was terrified, and he cried: 'Jesus nice, boy bach going to Capel is here. Grand is your son in Sion. Amen.' Dennis hasted onward and he remembered that he had left his sack on the Tree, and when he came back with the sack, the shadow was no longer on the road. Then he weighed that which he had seen and heard, and he imagined that the flying creatures were his enemies in the dress of birds, that the shadow was the Ruler of Sion; that the birds and the Ruler were scheming to take from him all that he had. In the darkness of Glasgoed he lit a tallow candle and counted his sovereigns and separated them evenly into four lots. He discovered Madlen's legs and removed therefrom the woman's stockings, and he also drew off his own stockings, and in each stocking he placed his money as he had divided it. Before he set out to bury his gold in four different parts, he cut his beard close to his skin, so that none of his enemies should know him. At dawn he brought forth his money and hid it in fresh quarters; and throughout that day he numbered and renumbered his cattle and his pigs and his hens, and he thought out the value of his crops. That night he would not go up to his bed. He cried out to Madlen: 'Where you was?'

'Hearing you am I, Dennis bach the husband,' Madlen said. 'Rest you, indeed.'

'Listen to my tongue.'

'Speak, then, boy bach.'

'Have the nice pigs eaten their fill?'

'Iss – iss.'

'Hungry are their sad grunts. Take food to them, you concubine.'

Madlen put barley meal into a bucket-full of skimmed milk and gave the pigs to eat.

'Wasteful you are, old female,' said Dennis. 'Bulging with potatoes is your stomach.'

'Only three, man bach, and a little buttermilk. Empty was my belly.'

'Not a yellow sovereign shall I have,' Dennis moaned. 'A wanton bitch you are.'

'Dennis bach, don't say!'

'Speak I so, iss-iss. Thin are the creatures, and you eat rare potatoes and buttermilk.'

Dennis opened the door of the lower end of his house and disturbed his hens which were roosting on the rafters. 'Is not the cheatful Rachel Hens coming tomorrow?'

'Don't you let your small guts worry you,' said Madlen. 'Fat enough are the hens.'

'Clap your mouth. Thin are the hens. Starving. Are not their bones like the blade of a scythe?'

Madlen stepped up to her bed. Dennis stayed at the door, and peered through the latch-hole. He wailed in this fashion: 'Two pitches of hay do I lose because of the dirty Mari.'

'Stiff is the head of the madam,' Madlen said. 'Herd her away with a rod. Put a pitchfork into her eyes.'

'Hist!' Dennis said. 'They are after my yellow sovereigns!' He stood on the threshold and spoke: 'Well, boys bach, what for are you here? Red money have I. No white silver. Religious boys bach you are. Iss-iss. Fair night, persons Capel Sion. Take you Madlen if her you desire. Do with her in the cow-house. Madlen, go now with the boys. No yellow sovereigns, indeed to goodness, have I. Did not my ass perish? . . . Madlen, a bitch you are. Tell them you did of the holes of my gold.'

'Safe is your large gold, Dennis bach,' Madlen replied.

'Told the boys you did. Robbed me you have.'

'Where have I robbed you?'

'Iss-iss. Spout the places of my yellow money? In the potato field?'

'No, Dennis, now –'

'In the rick? Bad if my rick fires this night.'

'Look you, sleep.'

'Where have you hidden my gold? Half one hundred sovereigns you have pilfered from me. All my sovereigns bach are gone. And their number was above the number of stones in the burial ground.'

Madlen shuddered: 'Wait small minutes.'

Dennis seized Madlen's body and he held it as one holds a battering ram and he beat the head against the wall, saying: 'Yellow sovereigns you have thieved. And red pennies. And white silver. My creatures' food is in your belly. An old thief you are. Two pitches of hay Mari spoiled. Two big pitches of my hay bach. Sorrowful is this. All are in array against me.'

He took a sheet from the bed and walked to the Field of the Tree, and he threw dry earth at Mari's window.

Mari answered: 'Boy bach come to court?'

Dennis moved to a place where Mari could not see him, for the moon was full, and he falsified his voice: 'Iss, now. Then, wench nice, come to the door.'

Mari arrived at the door and this is what she saw: a figure covered in a white sheet. She howled loudly and her mind became disordered.

In the evening of the day the young men and the young women coming home from the Seiet saw a shadow on the face of the Tramping road, and howsoever hard they searched no one could find a cause for it. They were disquieted. One cried at the top of his voice: 'A sign from the White Jesus bach!' and he sent three others to gather the most religious men in Sion to witness this thing. The religious men came and took counsel of one another, and the Respected Bern-

Davydd said: 'Blockheads you are, for sure. Find out we will what makes the old shadow.'

So the people walked hither and thither and in the fulness of time they came to the Field of the Tree, and from the tree hanged the body of Dennis Glasgoed. It was covered in a sheet and the wind swayed from side to side.

'Dennis, indeed, what for you do this?' said Ben Pensarn. 'The Fiery Pool is the cost of your sin.'

Davydd Bern-Davydd spoke: 'Like hogs do the wicked perish. Don't you touch the crow, Ben Pensarn. Your flesh is too saintly.'

Dennis hanged on the tree till the evening of the next day; as soon as the sun was down Ben called up to him two men, and he gave them a saw which had two handles, and he commanded them: 'Go you up and kill branch of the tree from which my sinful brother Dennis is hanging. Take you the rope fach from his neck and bring him whole to me. And carry a lantern with you, because tight is the knot that chokes a man. Be you careful you do not walk overmuch on the hay.'

The men felled the tree and took away the rope from Dennis's neck, and they carried the body on a wheelbarrow to Glasgoed and rested it on the floor by the body of Madlen.

At the return of day Ben Pensarn harnessed a horse into a cart, in the head of which he put Dennis's hens and in the back of which he put Dennis's pigs, and he drove to Castellybryn and sold the hens and the pigs. Thereafter he took possession of all that was Dennis's – except the gold which remains hidden – saying: 'My brother's keeper am I.'

# The Pillars of Sion

Silah Penlon was a doltish virgin. People who were bound to Capel Sion said to her mother:

'Large is the Big Man's curse upon you, Becws Penlon.'

'What for you speak wild, people bach?' answered Becws. 'Wench fach very tidy is the wench fach.'

The people rated her in a high voice. They said: 'Not pious is your brawl. There's vile is the blackhead of your mouth for you to talk like that.'

'Can I say, "Be you familiar indeed, then, Silah fach"?' Becws returned.

'What is the matter with the old woman? Tell me you!' cried the people. 'Full of sin was your old belly when you bore the wench. Explain, dear me, to us, Becws fach, the name of your sin and say longish prayers for you we will.'

Becws's spirit lowered: she was apprehensive that she would trespass unwittingly, and that the men who sat in the Big Seat in Capel Sion would inform against her to God. So she fashioned this prayer, which she spoke from time to time:

'Big Man bach, an old disorder you put on Silah. Do you lift him now from her. Wench fach very tidy is the wench fach also. Is she not a bulky age? Was she not born when the Respected Davydd Bern-Davydd came to Sion, thirty and five years ago? Stay with your son nice in the Capel and with all the boys bach of the Big Seat. Amen.'

God withheld His ear from Becws, and He fixed a further affliction to her daughter: He made Silah's mind stubborn and the virgin behaved as one who is dumb; and she would not entreat the Man of Terror to abate His anger against her. Becws was in fear and dread, and she bared her arm and stripped Silah and beat her; and the dirty spirits were strong within Silah, and though she wept she did not make any sound. Becws thought out another prayer, for her heart yearned for Silah: 'Speech Him advice to Becws fach Penlon, Big God. Solemn serious, act I will as He orders. Be near to His Son in Sion, and remain with the religious men of the High Places. Amen.'

In the night she dreamt that her goat had got dry without reason, and after she had punished her with the handle of a spade, a scarlet crow flew forth from out of the animal's mouth. Becws interpreted the dream thus: the goat was Silah, and the scarlet crow was the Bad Man from the Fiery Pool, and the handle of the spade was Bern-Davydd. Wherefore on the Sabbath she took out her funeral garments and put them on Silah, whom she brought into Sion; and mother and daughter sat among the hired people in the loft.

The rage of the congregation was high when they comprehended the meaning of this abomination.

'Ach y fi!' said one. 'A sick old mouse is Becws.'

'Out of her head is the female,' said another. 'Silah was conceived in brimstone. The dolt's hair is the colour of flames.'

The praying men said: 'Not right is this, people bach, dear me. Come, now, then, the most religious of us off will go and make phrases to the Respected.'

They went into the House of the Capel, and the chief of them was Amos Penparc, whose riches were above any other man on the floor of Sion, and whose piety was established. Amos stood on the threshold, and the lesser praying men stayed on the flagstone, which is without the door.

'Hello, here!' said Amos. 'Not wishful, religious Respected, are we to disturb his food eating, but there's grave are the words in my head.'

Bern-Davydd answered: 'Come you, boys bach Capel Sion,

the son of the Jesus bach will always hearken to you.'

'Well – well, then,' said Amos Penparc. 'What he does not know that Silah the mad bitch sat in Sion this day?'

'Indeed to goodness, Amos bach! Speak you like that, I shouldn't be surprised,' replied Bern-Davydd.

'And did I not observe the female Becws praying her own prayer while he was mouthing to the Great One?' said Amos.

'Don't speak any more, Amos Penparc,' said Bern-Davydd. 'Retch my old food I will. Read you the Speech Book for a small time bach.'

Bern-Davydd finished his eating, and he lifted his voice: 'Don't say!'

'Iss, iss, Respected.'

'Can a carrot turn colour?'

The praying men were amazed.

Amos Penparc said: 'Is not Silah counted an offender in the Palace of White Shirts?'

'Smell is Silah in the Big Man's nose,' said Bern-Davydd.

'Iss, little Respected,' said Amos. 'Fall upon us He will. He will smoulder our little ricks of hay. Speak him then what shall our cattle eat.'

At the close of the day Bern-Davydd, in the presence of all the congregation, addressed the men of the Big Seat: 'Now, then, boys Capel Sion, make proof about Silah the daughter of Becws. Amos Penparc, start, man bach.'

'Well, now, indeed, no,' said Amos. 'Right that the Religious of the Pulpit says sayings.'

'Much liking has the Big Man for you Amos,' said Bern-Davydd.

Amos rose and turned his bland countenance and unclouded his eyes upon the assembly, and fastening his coat over his beard, he spoke: 'Important in my pride is Sion. In Sion the Big Man's son dwells.' Then sang Amos Penparc: 'Lord bach, lessen your fury and depart not from us. Has not the Respected made us very religious? Is not the Capel like a well-stocked farm? The seating places are as full as the stables of the Drovers' Arms on an old fair day. And there's rising will be from the burial ground when Gabriel bach blows his gold trumpet: there will come up more people than I have sheep on the moor. Good is the Big Male to his photographs.' Amos ceased his song. 'But, people bach, sinful was Becws to bring her mad harlot into Sion. Lots of talk nasty there will be. Can corn grow from the seed of wasteful old thistles? Are mad bitches a glory unto Sion? How says the Respected: "Bad old smell in the Big Man's nose is Silah"? The Temple must be cleansed, indeed, now.'

'Wholesome, male man of Penparc, are your words,' said the Respected Bern-Davydd. 'Close my eyes I will now and say affairs to the Big Man: Jesus bach, wise you are to be with Amos Penparc. Full of wisdom is Amos, and his understanding is higher than the door of Sion, deeper than the whiskers under his waistcoat. Four pillars hold up the loft of Capel Sion, and not one is as strong as Amos. Lias Carpenter can hew the pillars with his saw, but who can hew through Amos? Speak now to us about cleaning the Temple. Mad is Silah, and did not Becws her mother bring her into Sion? Disgrace very bad is this. Lewd was the wench's behaviour, Jesus. Busy am I thinking out sermons, so you come down and tell orderings to Amos Penparc. Amen.'

Bern-Davydd's praise of Amos Penparc was spread abroad, whereof Becws got ashamed of that which she had done.

'Why you are without sense, idiot?' she said to Silah.

Silah did not answer.

'The concubine fach!' said Becws. 'A full barrow of sin is in your inside. Open your neck, you bull calf. Have you not made me wicked in the sight of Sion?'

Becws was angry that her daughter was speechless and she did not give her food for two days, and as Silah was yet stubborn she placed her in the pigsty and tied her hands together behind her back so that she could not open the door, and she said to her: 'Stay here, you scarlet crow; eat from the trough and lie with the swine.'

Silah licked from the trough, and lay with the pigs. The people had tidings of her punishment. Some came and hid in secret places about Penlon, and they came away and bore witness how that they had heard her babbling in this fashion to the pigs: 'Pigs bach, fetch a little barrow and take away the sin from my inside. Is there a haywaggon large enough to hold the sins of Bern-Davydd?'

'Take you no record, dear hearts, of the jolt-headed wench,' Becws pleaded with them. 'Without sense she is.'

The people noised Silah's blasphemy, and Becws removed her daughter from the pigsty, for she was afraid that the dirty spirits would go in and possess the swine.

'Come you into the house, you yellow pig,' she said. 'And clap your lips about the terrible Bern-Davydd. Is not Amos Penparc discussing you with Jesus?'

Silah did as she was commanded, and she was as dumb as she was before.

Amos addressed the congregation of the Seiet: 'Well – well, with God have I been. The Big Man came to the side of my bed. "Why for is your small face so down, Amos Penparc?" He said. "Have I withheld your crops or have I displeased you?" "Not for myself am I so low," I answered. "For sure, no, son bach. Has not the Respected reported well of you to me?" He said. "Grand preacher is Bern-Davydd," I talked. "Say you quick in a hurry what is the matter with you. Don't rouse my temper," He ordered. "Sion is foul." I sobbed, little people. And I told him how the mad bitch Silah had sat in the loft. Surprised was the Big Man. "Boy bach, you don't mean!" He cried. "Iss, indeed, old Silah Penlon made joy of her conception and I put my finger on the child in her belly." "Dear me!" I said. "Iss, Amos bach; say you to the Capel that the evil wench must cleanse the saintly abode, even the roof of the Temple. But she must not go up into my son's pulpit."'

The religious men answered Amen.

Silah came to free Sion of her filth, and Becws was with her; and in the middle of the day Amos Penparc entered to look into Silah's labour, and he was not pleased that Becws was there also.

'Why don't you obey, you strumpet born of a donkey?' he

cried in his wrath. 'Hard is your head. Cheating the Big Man of His price you are.'

Thereafter Amos tended Silah in Sion, and watched that she did not go up into the pulpit.

The morrow of the tenth day after the day that Silah had begun to clean Sion, the congregation gathered in the burial ground to bury the body of a man, and as the people looked down upon the floor of the grave, behold, the earth was disturbed and there were foot-holes in the walls of it. The people were abashed and awed, because the dead man had lived without reproach. They drew to Amos Penparc, asking of him: 'Amos the wise, make you explanations how this thing has come about.' Amos exercised his mind. He replied: 'A daughter of the Bad Man is in the Capel, and the last night old Satan came up from the Fiery Pool to converse with her.'

'Sober, indeed,' said one, 'did the black Satan enter the Capel? How now?'

Amos admonished this person: 'Like a squirrel of an infidel you are. Sion would consume Satan.'

In the middle of the twelfth week Sion was whole again. That which the Big Man had said to Amos Penparc was come to pass. All of the congregation were very proud. The praying men blessed the Lord, and the singing men and women sang His fame.

On a night Bern-Davydd assembled the men of the Big Seat, and to them he said: 'Boys bach, religious we are in Sion. Fitting now will be to show respect to the Big Man. Amos Penparc, give advice to us.'

'"Search the Scriptures," say the Book of Words,' Amos answered. 'Grand will be to hold a Questioning the Problem gathering. Little ruler, he will be the questioner.'

Sion took Amos's counsel and ordained this religious feast on the Day of Christmas, which was three months away; and the men cunning and subtle in the Word were bidden to the loft of Capel Sion to have their knowledge tested by Bern-Davydd.

As the day of the feast came near, Silah's size enlarged.

Becws was uneasy; she moaned on the Tramping road that her daughter was possessed of many satans. Moreover she heated an iron rod with fire and laid it on Silah's navel. But the satans did not go away; and Silah's size continued to increase.

Now in the dark Silah left her mother's house and journeyed through the fields to Penparc, and at the door of the stable she made a noise like the bray of a mule. Amos came out to her and opened the door of the stable, and he said to her: 'Now, well-well, Silah Penlon, how was you, then?'

Silah put out her arms and drew Amos to her; and she uttered words: 'Boy bach nice is Amos.' Amos was dismayed and he could not free himself from her embrace. Before the darkness got thin he laid a snare for her: 'Come you here before the twilight of the third day, Silah fach, and a large little reward will I give you. Go you out, now, through the little window.'

Silah went abroad in the neighbourhood and she laughed in the face of the people and spoke foolishly in their hearing. She was joyous, though she did not know anything. Becws thanked the Lord loudly: was He not repenting of His works against Silah?

On the eve of the twilight of the third day Silah stood at the door of the stable of Penparc and she made a noise like the bray of a mule. Amos came out of his house and there was with him Bern-Davydd, and to him he said: 'What's that old shouting, I don't know?' and they two walked up to Silah.

Bern-Davydd seeing her, said: 'Go you off, you mad bitch of hell fire.'

Silah did not attend to his words. She put out her arms. 'Boy bach nice is Amos Penparc,' she cried.

Amos was vexed. 'What for you mean, you clobstick?' he said. 'Religious, witness him that I am falsely accused.'

'What you call?' said Bern-Davydd to her. 'Away you off now, or for sure kick your teeth will I.'

As Silah did not move Bern-Davydd threw her upon the ground. The woman rose, turned, and ran. Bern-Davydd and

Amos followed her and pelted her with stones, and with clods of earth. At Penlon, Amos said to Becws: 'Shout you up your swine Silah.'

Silah came.

'Deny, you cow,' said Amos to her, 'that I have been bad with you. Jesus bach, if I have mixed my flesh with the flesh of any old female, make you a small sign.'

He gazed around for a sign, and here was none; and he congratulated the Big Man that He was on the side of righteousness.

Then he counselled with Bern-Davydd, and they two caused a seat to be set for Silah in the cow-stall, and they placed over her neck a hempen halter, the ends of which were attached to an iron staple driven deep into the wood of the stall.

Silah bit through the rope and thieved the saw of Lias Carpenter, and she came by stealth into Capel Sion, and sawed through each of the four pillars; and no one saw her going in or coming out. In the morning the subtle men congregated in the loft. The pillars parted, and the loft fell, but Amos Penparc was without hurt.

# The Deliverer

Although Job Stallion was instructive in prayer and joyous in song, he was without esteem in Sion. The place of his abode was Cwmcoed, which is on the land that rises from the other side of Avon Bern, and the name of his mother was Peggi; and they two had a maid-servant whose name was Hetti. Job searched among the women of Sion and among the women who frequented the fairs of Castellybryn for a wife who would free Cwmcoed from the mortgage which Amos Penparc held upon it; of the daughters of Sion and of the women who went to the fairs none would wed him because all had knowledge of his state. This also was spoken: 'Hetti is breaking her hire. Thick is the wench by Job.'

One day Amos came to Cwmcoed. Peggi saw him from a long way off, and she shouted to Job: 'The old scamp Amos is after yellow money.'

Job joined Amos in the lower field, and he was moved to say to him: 'Like the happy Apostle, indeed, man, who walked with the White Jesus, I feel.'

Amos gave no understanding to Job's words, and he said: 'Speech have I for you, Job Cwmcoed.'

'Well-well, now?'

'Wounded am I to speak. That smallish bit of money. Job, dear me, repay you the yellow ones.'

'Not meaning you was; say you now,' said Job.

'Why for you speak lightly?' answered Amos. 'In mouthing does not my neck get dumb?'

'Ho, ho. Thus, indeed, then.'

'Old money must I have, Job.'

'Give money I would if I had him.'

Job cried to his mother Peggi: 'Serious, old mam, Amos Penparc wants his money.'

There was much earth in the crevices of Peggi's face, and her body was bent from service on the land, and she shivered when she heard the words of her son: she seemed like a sapless tree which harbours every refuse that the wind blows.

'Solemn is this,' she said. 'Sell the stallion bach you must, Job.'

'Religious you speak, little woman,' answered Amos. 'Does not the Book of Words say to us to pay our debts? There's bad would I be to speak to Daniel Auctions: "Go, sell Cwmcoed".'

Job was enraged with his mother that she had borrowed money from Amos Penparc, and he told her that her life was a heavy load upon him. Peggi was too old to weep: she made yowling sounds.

In the evening she craved Job's forgiveness. 'Woe to us,' she moaned, 'that we are on top of Amos's old finger.'

Job was aroused out of his sluggishness, for he was in narrow straits, and he meditated: he planned to go to the Market of Carmarthen, where he was a stranger, to seek a wife among the women who gathered there. Hence the sixth day, which was the Day of the Market, he made himself to appear gay: he clothed himself grandly in cloth garments, and he covered his crooked legs with cloth leggings; he combed the hairs which were on his cheeks, and he put a bowler hat on his head.

Then he ordered Peggi to saddle for him the pony and to bring the animal to the gate of the close. Peggi did accordingly; and when he was on the pony, she spoke: 'Don't you now, heart bach, be tempted by a bad girl on account of her looks. Beware of fair women. Go court a wench whose nice purse is as big as a fatted bullock's belly.'

'Spout like a bull you do,' Job answered. 'What is the matter with the root of your tongue? Why don't you clap up the backhead of your neck?'

'Close you must, Job bach,' Peggi persisted. 'Shall the cow Amos take away our farm?'

'Hie off,' said Job, 'and suck your toes.'

Job rode away; and on his journey he fixed his mind: if Cwmcoed were taken from him he would be called a fool in Sion. Sell the stallion bach he could, but the cost would not pay all of that which was borrowed from Amos. Did not the red mackerel say: 'Glad am I to lend you money, Peggi fach?' Dear me to goodness, what a black the old snail was. Tight, dear me, was Amos. Good, now, if Jesus bach smote him with a flame of fire like He did the Unitarian infidel in Castellybryn. Job also explained to the Lord how that the borrower should be the payer; how that Cwmcoed and all the land thereto, and all that was in the land and on it was his if Peggi took wing.

Outside Shop Llewellyn Shones he magnified his holdings in the presence of Enoch Boncath – a man of twenty-five heads of cattle and one hundred and twenty acres of good land – and after he had boasted for a long while he said: 'Misther Enoch bach, say you what now if I looked merry on your female daughter Ann.'

Misther Enoch was unfamiliar with Troedfawr and the land and the people in that neighbourhood, and inasmuch as Ann was stricken by the disease king's evil, he replied: 'Open your throat to the damsel. Go now to the House of the Market and say to her: "Talked have I to your father."'

Job came down to Ann, who was sitting on the ground; her legs were crossed, as a tailor crosses his legs, and her outer skirt, which was of black cloth, was drawn up so that she sat on her scarlet flannel petticoat; and before her was a tub of butter. Her right cheek was marked by the malady which was upon it, and around her neck she had a band of calico which was wet with the moisture that drained from her wound.

'In private I will counsel in your ears, Ann Boncath,' said Job.

'Comic one you are, man,' replied Ann. 'Speak for what.'

A toothless woman, who sat by Ann, spoke: 'Very quiet the stable of the Red Cow is, indeed to goodness.'

A dealer drove his testing scoop into Ann's butter, and he bought it. Ann rose, and as she passed away the toothless woman said: 'Give the wench one of rocks Mari.'

Job took Ann up to Mari Rocks, and he purchased for her a sweetmeat, and as the custom is, Ann did likewise for him; and the people around and about observed that which was done, and remarked: 'Boy bach, great shall be your courting this night.' To Ann they said: 'Very catching now is king's evil.'

They two walked out of the town and into a field. Presently Job said: 'I will go and make a league with Misther Enoch your father.'

And Job passed into the town to make a league with Ann's father, and after he had said many pleasing words, he said this of himself: 'Wonderful is my religious fame in Sion. Honouring your girl am I to take her into Cwmcoed.'

'Glad is your speech, boy bach,' replied Misther Enoch. 'Yet now just not no nor yea can I say. Come will I and spy over Cwmcoed.'

At the middle of the next day Job came home and he told his mother everything. Peggi's mind cherished vengeance; she gazed across the valley to the parcel of trees in the midst of which is Penparc; and her sight tried to pierce the mist which covered the Hills of Boncath, from whence was to come her deliverer. She petted Job, for she knew that he had established his right to Ann; and she served him with broth and pancakes; and Job, having eaten his fill, slept. She designed to go to Penparc and say slyly to Amos: 'Here, male bach, is your ugly money. Take you the small sum: hap you want him largely. Sorry I am you are so poor. May he give you a yellow heart. Horrible were the words of the Big Man about the Calf of Gold."

She designed further: on the coming of Ann she would go into Shop Rhys and buy soap, and she would clean herself with soap and water and rest from toil. She would name herself headwoman of Cwmcoed – the mistress would say to Ann: 'Do you this' and 'Do you that,' and Ann should be as a servant in her house.

In the folly of her gladness, she showed malice against Hetti: 'Move your heavy body, you large trollop.'

'Peggi, dear me,' said Hetti. 'This one minute, do I not suffer pains then? An old child bach is about to come.'

The words incensed Peggi: 'Sober me, why for you did not say you were thick? Run you home, you nasty harlot. Is not Enoch Boncath and his daughter Ann coming on the sixth day to view the land?'

Hetti excited her spirit: 'And say to Ann Boncath will I that this is Job's child.'

Old Peggi was dispirited that moment, and she feared for her schemes. She tore out from a hedge two slight twigs, which she coupled together, and with which she punished the servant woman. Hetti fell forward, whereupon Peggi raised the maid's garments and beat the flesh of her body.

At first Hetti made a great noise, then she became silent, and Peggi knew that there was no more spite left in her.

Her body grievous, Hetti walked out and up into the loft which is over the stable and gave birth to a child. The afternoon of the second day she returned to the living house, and she looked oddly as she held up her infant before Peggi's eyes. 'Peggi, the female fach,' she said, 'who is this that has come from Edom?'

Thuswise Peggi was consoled that the Lord had not deserted her. She said to herself: 'Very tidy is the little Big One to His children bach.' To Hetti she said: 'Mad you are, the wicked animal. Go you away.'

Hetti bared her bosom and pressed her child's head against her breast; and in that fashion she walked along the Roman road and over the heather to her mother's house – which is on the top of the hill that goes down into Morfa. She did not harass either Peggi or Job afterwards.

On the sixth day Enoch Boncath arrived to search out the

land and to establish by questions that Job had not exalted anything; and to all his questions Peggi devised deceitful answers; and Job moreover showed him fat pasture that was beyond the boundary of Cwmcoed, saying: 'Iss – iss, that is our land, boy bach.' But Enoch was cunning and he inquired of strangers; one answered him: 'Job, dear me, is a tardy old sow. All, look you, his land is wasted. And does not Peggi owe much yellow money to Amos Penparc?' Enoch pondered the sayings which were told him for ten days, and then he came to Cwmcoed to speak abusively. Having delivered his speech, he said: 'Send Sheremia Polis Boncath I will after you.'

Job strengthened his spirit and feigned anger. He said: 'Male out of his head are you; and there's a scamp.'

'Iss, for sure me,' said Peggi. 'Behave you do like a colt.'

'Count the days you can,' said Job, 'that Ann will display her thickness.'

'Out of sin has come the disease of your wench,' cried Peggi. 'Did not Job wash his body when he came home?'

'Dark is your talk,' Enoch said. 'The damsel fach is all right.'

Enoch journeyed home, and on his way he thought on the sayings of Peggi and Job; and every day he said this to Ann: 'How you was?'

'So and so are things with me, father bach,' Ann at last answered him.

'Well – well, bad black is Job Stallion.' Enoch came out of his house; he told no one of the place whither he was bound, and so that none could imagine his purpose he walked through field paths and lanes. He reached Cwmcoed at the milking hour.

'Come have I yet again,' he said.

'My boy bach has turned his mind,' said Peggi, 'and he is throwing gravel indeed at the window of a fine ladi. Male frolicsome is Job.'

'Say you like that,' said Enoch. 'Sad am I that I spoke quickly to you. Ann wants to wed Job.'

'What for does Job need an unhealthy wench? No – no, man. Go home, Enoch Boncath: busy am I preparing for the marriage.'

'Woman fach,' Enoch said, 'be not hard now. Ten yellow sovereigns and six cheeses will Ann bring with her.'

'Empty is your voice,' said Peggi.

'And there's a one she is for making butter.'

'Good-bye, Enoch Boncath, and good-bye to your thick Ann.'

'Fifteen yellow sovereigns will Ann bring with her, and a waggon-load of hay.'

'Three hundred is the number of yellow sovereigns that Job will get with his wench,' said Peggi.

Job entered the milk shed; his mother said to him: 'Old Enoch Boncath is here. There's a big pleader he is, for sure me.'

'Waggle your tongue,' said Job.

'One very high you are in Sion, Job Cwmcoed,' said Enoch. 'Be you religious and take Ann my female daughter.'

Job and Peggi goaded Enoch so that he became as one who is drunk; and it came to be that Ann settled in Cwmcoed and her marriage dowry was two hundred sovereigns, a cow in calf and a heifer, a plough, a bed, and a load of hay; and when she was settled she saw that the land was indeed barren by neglect and that rust was on many of the implements. As the time of the birth of her child came near, her malady grew worse and it ruffled her temper, and she hated Peggi and Job because of their guile.

'Get up, you hare of the Fiery Pool,' she cried to Peggi in the darkness before the dawn.

'No – no. The dawn is not grey yet,' Peggi whimpered.

Ann removed the cloths which covered her mother-in-law and dragged her down from the bed.

The old woman rose from the ground: 'Headwoman am I. Go out and labour, you concubine.'

Ann gave no mind to Peggi's words; but she reviled Job because of her.

'A rotten old woman is my mam,' said Job.

Howsoever Peggi contrived, she did not become the headwoman of Cwmcoed; she was made to labour in the outhouses and on the land, to sleep on a straw mattress in the straw loft;

she never changed her garments, and earth and dung fastened to the material thereof like sun-dried clay. She clung to her life through the summer and the autumn of the year; in the winter she lost it and was buried in the burial ground of Capel Sion; and in her agony there was none to comfort her or to minister unto her. Job also Ann forced to labour all the light hours; and though he murmured against her tyranny, he obeyed her in all things. In his perplexity he plotted mischief against her, and plotted he never so constant, Ann would not abate any of the rigour of her dealings with him. He was as a hired man in Sion, and without dignity in his house. His state vexed him greatly. He brooded over Ann's harshness, and he planned a scheme by which he would win an advantage over his wife: he dampened the feather bed on which she slept. Having done that, he said: 'I shall not lie with you any more, for your disease stinks.'

He dampened the bed many times, and the day came that Ann went up to her bed to be delivered of her third child. She became very sick, and died. Job put a White Shirt on her, and at her open grave he wept and said: 'Big Man, forgive this woman: fond of old money she was and very nasty she was to mam fach.' Then he prayed a prayer which he had rehearsed, and raised his singing voice in a holy hymn.

# *Judges*

After Essec Penparc was buried John Tyhen would not give over the meadow to his brother Amos, although that it was a portion of Amos's inheritance from Essec, and although that in the face of the congregation Amos stood at his father's grave and proclaimed that his patrimony was just. Of that John took no heed, for the man's manners were harmful: he performed service on his land on the Sabbath, and his Sabbath garments were not respectful unto Sion, and he coveted temporal possessions. So it was that Amos came down to the Shepherd's Abode, and spoke to the Respected Bern-Davydd:

'Do him forgive me, little Preacher. Don't him think me insulting or irreligious that I come here in my worldly clothes. Heavy is my spirit – heavier than the grand stone I'm putting at the head of my father's grave. And to whom shall I go for counsel bach if not to the Respected?'

'Amos, dear me,' said Bern-Davydd, 'the Judge of Sion is righteous, man.'

'Sanctimonious he is, religious one,' said Amos.

'Put your backhead on a stool, Amos son of Essec, and shake your tongue.'

'Indeed, down is my spirit, little man. Is not John plotting against me because my father gave me the meadow?'

'Amos, Amos. Not speaking serious you are.'

'Iss. Disheartening are the words John shouts of me.'

'Don't be vexed, Amos the one good. Very harshly will the Man of Terror deal with John.'

'Bad now that a brother reviles a boy bach like me.'

Bern-Davydd sang: 'Where's the old profit though the black gains the meadow and loses his White Shirt? Not his knife, nor his trousers. Not his wheelbarrow, nor his clogs. But his soul, male bach. Terrible Man, smite the blackguard John. Speech to me, little boy, the rent of the meadow.'

'Well – well, small is the money, for sure. Angry would the Big Man be if I mouthed nay to my father's blessing.'

'Wise you are, boy. Go forth will I and hold inquisition over the sow and lord it over him. Explain the bigness of the meadow.'

'Of acres two; of worry a cartload.'

'Loss awful to Capel Sion when Essec flew. Go you to his place in the Big Seat.'

'Holy that will be.'

'Ask the Great Judge will I how to deal with John,' said Bern-Davydd. 'The meadow is worth two sovereigns a year, shall I spout?'

'No – no, Respected Peacher bach.'

'Is he worth a sovereign and half a sovereign?'

'No – no, man. No, indeed.'

'Don't be jokeful, Amos. Speak.'

'One small yellow sovereign, Preacher nice.'

'Ho – ho. A slip of a miser is John. And he is a worse old thief than his cat. Look you, we will tell against him.'

Bern-Davydd called on his wife Sara, and he said to her: 'Bring you my preaching coat, and my cuffs, and fasten you my collar about my neck, and put on my feet the elastic boots.'

Then he said to Amos: 'Come, Amos Essec. Let us go up to the mountain.'

When they reached the top of the moor, Bern-Davydd made an utterance. This is that which he uttered: 'Not saintly enough are you to come into the Big Man's presence. Tarry you here while I climb the mound to hold forth.' Before he departed, he emptied his mouth of its spittle and laid the pellet of tobacco that was in his mouth on a stone: and so with a clean mouth he reported to God. Presently he came down, and he replaced the tobacco, and took the india-rubber cuffs from off his wrists and the collar from off his neck.

'Amos the dirty son of Essec,' he said, 'sin has come from your throat. Ach y fi, the awful swine. Scrape her with a shovel. Why for you say that the meadow is worth a yellow sovereign?'

'Little Respected,' Amos answered, 'I said that in my littleness. Wishful I was to hide John's avarice. Forgive him his servant.'

'Shut your head. Thus saith the Big Man: "Costly is the meadow, Bern bach, at a yellow sovereign."'

'And like that the Big Man?'

'Thus saith the Large Farmer: "See you, photograph, that Amos keeps the meadow, for is he not Essec's blessing to him?"'

'Amen, Bern-Davydd bach religious.'

'The Man of Vengeance saith: "Tell you Amos that you will rent the meadow from him for one half a yellow sovereign to be paid on the day of the Hiring Fair. Of the grass that grows there the pony that carries you about and about to preach preaches shall eat."'

'Don't he say!' cried Amos, and he doubled up his beard and put the end thereof into his mouth. He mumbled: 'Do I not need the meadow for my cows? Is he not the best grazing land hereabout? Be him sensible, boy religious of the pulpit.'

Thereat Bern-Davydd pitched his voice: 'Will you be as evil as John? Will you dispute with the Big Man?' He also appointed a set time, saying: 'Such and such a day I shall take God's pony into the meadow. Hie you away and order John.'

Amos said yea, because the close friendship between Bern-Davydd and the Big Man awed him. It was that in the dimness of the day he entered the field in which John and John's wife Martha were toiling, and he said: 'Very messy is things after the old rain, little people.'

John looked at his brother: 'Why for you say extraordinary?'

'A mess, too, is life without the Palace of White Shirts,' Amos replied. 'Longish were the prayers I made this day.'

'Talk a plain talk, Amos,' said John.

'Rented the field bach have I to Bern-Davydd.'

'Dear glory me, for why you act so strangely?'

'Was I not thinking of you, my brother, and of you, my sister?' answered Amos. 'Grieved am I that you labour so hardly.'

'Old man nasty you are to rent what is not yours.'

'Hold your words, John bach,' said Amos. 'What does the Apostle say about kicking against the pricks? And did I not speak over the grave of father Essec that the meadow was mine?'

John remembered: by the sweat of his limbs he kept profitable the twenty acres of gorse land attached to Tyhen; he tilled and digged and drained, and his body was become crooked and the roots of his beard were caked with some of the earth that had enabled him to gather much wealth, even seventy sovereigns. He struck Amos.

'Meek am I in my religion,' said Amos. 'Above all the men on the face of the earth, I am the most humble.' He turned upon his brother his cheek.

That night John set a clamp to the gate of his meadow so that no one could enter the field; and as he came back to Tyhen, he saw his cat eating the herring that remained from the midday meal.

'You wasteful daughter of a robin,' he cried to his wife Martha. 'There's bad you are. Why did you not hide the fish? Was he not as large as my leg? He would make the next day's meal also.'

He went out and caught the cat and brought it into the house; and he called up to him Martha and his two children, and he laid the animal on the table and in their sight he killed it. He divided the carcase into two, and one piece he nailed in the door of Penparc, and one piece he nailed in the door of the Shepherd's Abode.

# The Day of Judgment

The respected Bern-Davydd proclaimed against John Tyhen in Sion: 'Boys, boys, there's an awful black for you. Half an old cat he pegged on my door the last night. Sober serious. Mishtress Bern-Davydd saw the filth. "Keep him silent for a time bach," she said, "while I retch from my belly." Words to the Big Man will I now sound.'

This is Bern-Davydd's report: 'A fulbert is John Tyhen, for sure me. Tempted was his father Essec by an old servant wench, and the iobess spat John. Easier for you to thread a camel with large horns and three humps through the eye of a stocking needle than for a bastard slip to pass into the Palace of White Shirts. Why isn't John like his half-brother Amos Penparc? Man very religious and wise is Amos, and much money he possesses. Go I did and say to Amos: "Grass the pony that belongs to the photograph of the Big Man must have." "Take him the meadow that is in the hiring of John Tyhen," answered Amos. And John was angry that Amos gave to the Large One. He slayed his cat, and one half of him he nailed on the door of the Shepherd's Abode and half on the door of Penparc. Mishtress Bern-Davydd is not flopped on her pew on this Sabbath of Bread and Wine, little people. Why for not? At the finish of her retch she lamented: "Bern-Davydd, the Bad Man is closer than the Big Man. Not eat of the Flesh or drink of the Blood will I until the Bad One is beaten into stones as small as gravel." What a speech, boys bach! This day the Judge said to me: "Bern bach, have John Tyhen afflicted by the Seiet on the third night. I will set stiffness in his heart, and your messengers shall lay hands on the red frog. This would I do myself, but how can my white fingers play the Harp fach after touching the stinkard?"'

Bern-Davydd descended into the Big Seat and uncovered the bread and wine; the congregation ate and drank, and then he prayed:

'Well, Big King bach, glad are boys Sion that you have commanded them to bring John to the Seiet. Much will be the muster. If the bullock is obstinate send rats into his house, and vermin into the inside of his cattle, and rot his crops. Leave you the meadow. Good is the grass and very benefitful for the pony of your religious son. Amen, little White Jesus. Amen.'

The people said: 'Amen.'

When all the congregation had heard of that which John had done against Bern-Davydd, the valiant men arose to do him hurt, and these are the chief men who gathered between the evening lights at the gate of the Garden of Eden: Davydd Bern-Davydd, Ben the Keeper of the House of the Capel, Lloyd Schoolin' who is the beginner of the singing in Sion, Abel Shones Poor Relief who is the most spiritual of all the praying men on the floor of Sion, Old Ianto of the Road who is the grave-digger, and Amos Penparc, whose riches in land and money are above those of any in the land. There were also many old women and young, and old men and young.

Now of they who presumed to fall upon Tyhen: Bern-Davydd and Abel Shones went into Sion to pray; Amos Penparc rested on the roadside because his clogs were new and hurtful, and he would have help from no one; moreover, when the procession neared Tyhen, some faltered, for they had understanding of the spirit of John.

Lloyd Schoolin' was the first to enter Tyhen. John was repairing the nose of his plough, and Martha his wife was suckling her infant and stirring the pigs' food which was heating in a cauldron over the peat and wood fire.

'Indeed, now, dear me,' said Lloyd, 'come you two at once to the Seiet.'

'Well – well,' John answered. 'Come would I, but the plough bach I must use tomorrow.'

'We don't use ploughs in the Palace, John,' said Lloyd. 'Why babble you like a blockhead?'

'Say you like that,' replied John.

'Irreligious you are, man. Indeed to goodness, shift, and put on your trousers cloth.'

John raised his face and these words came through his broken lips: 'The cows are not milked and the pigs are hungry. Look after affairs must I. Large was the cost of the coffins of my two children who perished.'

'Male Tyhen,' cried Lloyd, 'the Big Man calls you to account. A goat was you to sin against the Respected.'

'Why then did he steal my meadow?'

'By the mouth of Bern-Davydd, the Man of Terror orders you to Sion,' said Lloyd.

'Fair night, boys bach,' John answered.

Martha counselled her husband: 'Obey, John bach. Warn you did I against gathering in the hay on the Sabbath. Go, now, and take a nice hen fach to the Respected.'

'Shut down your neck,' John admonished his wife.

A woman of Sion pressed her yellow face close to the suckling infant, and as she spoke the loosened black tooth in her mouth trembled. 'Is this your child, John bach Tyhen?' she cried. 'Many have been with your hussy. Ach y fi, Shim Tinker is the father of the brat.'

'Don't say,' Martha pleaded. 'No strange man has known me.'

The men and women of Sion rounded John and Madlen; and the man they seized and took into the close, and having fastened him with a rope to his cart, they brought forth the woman and her infant.

Lloyd Schoolin' cried with a loud voice: 'This is Gomorrah. Children of wickedness must be cleansed.'

'Iss – iss,' the woman of Sion voiced.

'As dirty with smell they are as a hen loft,' said Lloyd. 'Wash the dung from their flesh.'

The pond of Tyhen is at the foot of the close, and into it the rains bring much of the residue from the cowhouse and the stable and the pigstye; and the water is still water.

John saw that he was put to worse before Sion.

'Persons, don't now,' he cried. 'Come with you will I. Drop dead and blind, come will I.'

The men unbound him and they drove him to the brim of the pond, and as he faltered one urged him with a hay fork. John walked through the pond; he was a high man and the water came to his knees. Martha's stature was little and the water lifted her garments as far as her thighs; Lloyd Schoolin' peered closely, and then opened his mouth, speaking in this sort: 'Boys bach, look you. She is not husband-high to John. Wet she will be for Shim Tinker.'

Thereafter John and Martha were taken to Capel Sion, and they were made to stand under the pulpit, which is in the eye of the congregation.

Amos Penparc rose in the Big Seat, and turned his face to the people, saying: 'Little sons and daughters of the Big Man bach, true that John has made himself my enemy, but very forgiving am I to those who curse me. See you, here is the piece of turk-cat he nailed on my door. Still, I forgive the bull-calf. Am I not saintly and full of religion? The loutish rabbit sinned against the Big Man's son. There's merciful is the Respected that he didn't say to God: "John Tyhen is at my door. Kill him with an axe!" Remember you the old infidel who died in the Shire Pembroke? The Bad Man left the mark of his clog on his body. Deal you not too harshly with the bastard slip. Nor think the lighter of me for his sin. Have not the sayings of his iniquity made my ears tingle?'

Amos placed the carcase which was nailed in his door beside that which was nailed in the door of the Shepherd's Abode. 'There is your cat, Son of Satan,' he said. 'Say you why you did this vile thing.'

It was so that John's courage weakened, and he lied and

charged Martha with the fault, and he also called her to bear witness of his guiltlessness; and Martha, who calmed her infant's cries with her breast, said: 'Serious, my male knows nothing of the turk-cat. Go we will now. The cows are not milked, and a feeling of foreboding curdles my milk.'

'Wicked spider,' cried Lloyd Schoolin'. 'The Fiery Pool is curdling your milk. Respected, whip them with prickly speeches.'

'The night of yesterday,' said Bern-Davydd, 'the Big Man came to me in a White Shirt. "Bern-Davydd! Bern bach!" He called. "Big Man," I answered, "your photograph listens." Thus the Large One: "I will perform against John Tyhen all and more than I have spoken to you concerning him. Of him and Martha and their children and their cattle I will make an end. I will devour the robin's sovereigns and silver. Burning is my anger. Tell you the toad to make sacrifices unto Sion."'

'Glad would I be to give,' said John. 'A large little cabbage I will bring him.'

'Clap your mouth, fool,' cried Bern-Davydd. 'Why for you make messes when there was no mess to be?'

'Pilfer my meadow you did,' John answered, and he did not try to discourage the fury that was rising within him, for his heart was mean and he was covetous of all things.

'John bach,' said Martha, 'obey you the voice.'

'Why for must I toil for Bern-Davydd?' John replied. 'Do I starve for him? My two children perished and fat was the pig I gave for their coffins. Ask you Lias Carpenter. Lias, speak, man.'

Bern-Davydd closed his hearing with the tips of his fingers. 'Chase them out,' he commanded, 'like Big Jesus did the swine, or hap the roof will fall on my religious head.'

John and Martha were driven from Capel Sion. The valiant men and women followed them and stoned them to the door of Tyhen. That night, before the wicks were turned down in the lamps of the Temple, the children of Sion gloried that the Chapel was purged of sin; that they had done all that the Big

Man had commanded them to do by the tongue of His son Bern-Davydd...

Martha milked her cows and separated the cream from the milk and fed her pigs, and when her labour and the labour of John were ended, they two looked upon their infant, and behold it was dead; and the Bad Man had branded its forehead with the mark of a stone. John, humbled to rage, lifted his face and raised his voice: 'Cruel you are to me, God bach. Wasting much am I in burying the perished. Turn you your think, dear me, and put back the life into the wench fach. Be with your son in Sion. Amen.'

He waited for the performance of the miracle until the body stiffened. In the break of the day he sacrificed a lamb unto Sion.

# The Acts of Dan

Dan son of Shan – a servant in Pentremawr, which is against the shores of Morfa – on a day said to his master: 'Not wise that I labour for you. A photograph bach am I of the Big Man. How talk, then, if I say: "I break my hire"?'

He put his clothes and his clogs in a wooden box, and he carried the box to Groesfordd, which was the abode of his mother Shan and which is at the foot of the hilly road that goes up to the Moor. He assumed he was above all the religious men in Capel Sion, and in the Seiet he rose and exclaimed: 'Boys bach, a photograph of Big Man am I.'

The Respected Davydd Bern-Davydd denied him, saying: 'The fool is lame in the foot: old club is at the bottom of his leg, and light is the weight of his sense. Brawling evil is the iob. Shan fach, very grieved you are for your idiot. People, hear you Shan say now: "Indeed, iss, Religious Respected."'

Shan adored Dan. Her mind was elated that God had ceased His anger against her bastard son, and she prayed within her that the number of blessings He would heap upon Dan would be as the number of stones which marred her field. She muttered: 'Murmuring, dear congregation, is always the boy bach to the One in the sky. Large joy he makes of his religion.'

'Serious to goodness, off is your temper,' Bern-Davydd said. 'Lunatic is Dan. Boys Capel Sion, laugh provokingly at Dan Groesfordd. Know you all that I am the Big Man's photograph.'

The praying men – the first praying men who were in the Big Seat – laughed and answered as with one mouth: 'Words very well he speeches, Respected.' The lesser praying men – they whose seats were on the floor of Sion – did likewise.

Howsoever the people mocked and chided him, none was able to entreat Dan to humble himself or to give over his false argument. He stood in the public places and proclaimed that he was the Son of God, and he prophesied that he would prevail above Sion, that he was the chosen Ruler of the Pulpit.

One day he took a bucket into his mother's field and made a tinkling noise upon it, and he cried: 'Shoot! Shoot!' Thus he enticed up to him Shan's fattening pig. He seized the pig and carried it to the Garden of Eden. On the way thither he uttered with a great voice: 'Sinners Capel Sion, come you, children bach and gaze on what I do for the White Jesus nice. Awful is the religious dirt in your bellies.' He put the pig on the floor of the Garden and killed it. Then he discoursed to the people: 'Mountains of bad evil there is, boys. Did not the Big Ruler say to me: "Now, now, Dan Groesfordd, picture of me you are, man bach. Hie off, and slay Shan's pig in my name!"' Dan removed the pig to Groesfordd and Shan poured boiling water over it and scraped the hairs from off the skin, and when she had separated the carcase into small pieces, Dan said to her: 'Go now the next day and sell the pieces bach to the people. If one says to you: "Not wanting the flesh of pig do I" speak like this: "Buy now, for sure. Is not this the swine that perished in the Big Man's name?"'

Shan obeyed the order of her son Dan, and she did not turn her face until she had utterly sold the pig, even the entrails, and when she returned she said to Dan: 'Love bach of my heart, take you the yellow gold and white silver.' She spread three shawls on the floor and rested upon them.

For two days Dan hid from the people, and he would not eat or drink anything. He came forth from his hiding place and lamented at the Gates of Sion: 'Old mam fooled me to sell the corpse of the Big Man's pig. Stinging is my spirit. Ugly are the sovereigns and shillings she gave me. Accursed mam have I. And has not the Big One said: "Dan bach, Jesus is on my right hand, and you are on my left hand"?'

As he was speaking a stranger woman, who was very large, stopped the horse that was between the shafts of her cart, and spoke to Dan these words: 'What does the boy bach say?'

'Woman from where are you?' Dan answered.

'Ho, ho, the mishtress of Blaenpant am I.'

'Puzzling you are,' said Dan. 'Where shall I say is Blaenpant?'

'O, well – well. In Conwil.'

'Enlarge your mouth and tell the name of you and your man. There's sly you are to keep secrets.'

'Is not my name Sali Blaenpant? Gone is the husband to the Palace of White Shirts.'

'Dear me,' said Dan. 'Dear me. Abide do I with the Big Man. Not anything concerns me but Him.' Then sang Dan Groesfordd: 'Sali Blaenpant, is not the Big Man the landlord of all the fields? Even the land under the old potatoes He owns. Good He is to ones religious and bad to unbelievers. He did say to me: "Dan bach, don't you now let an old razor touch the hairs of your face, because I will make a photograph of the White Jesus bach." A great pig I sacrificed and my Satan of Mam sold the saintly corpse. What for you say to that?'

'Serious sin,' Sali the stranger woman answered; 'give you a suckling pig will I.'

'Stout, Sali Blaenpant, the pig was,' said Dan. 'To the Big Man you give a stout little pig.'

Sali addressed her horse: 'Gee, old mare fach. Good-bye, boy nice, and good-bye again'; and she departed believing. She spoke of that which she had seen and heard, saying: 'The second Jesus is Dan Groesfordd.' She sent to Dan a letter, in which she wrote that he was greater than all the rulers.

Dan journeyed to Blaenpant.

'How you was then?' he said to Sali.

'Very good, thanks be to you, religious boy.'

'Much land you have here,' said Dan.

'One hundred acres but ten acres,' said Sali.

'Well and well,' said Dan. 'An old bother is a mortgage.'
'Iss, boy bach. But there's no mortgage on Blaenpant.'
'Happy you are in your offences,' said Dan. 'What will Blaenpant profit you in the Palace of White Shirts? Give did I all to the Big Man. Speechify religion will I now. This is what the Angel said to me the first night: "Grand for you to preach preaches in a Capel."'
'Wise was the Angel,' said Sali.
'Poor am I in silver and gold,' said Dan, 'and rich in religion. How say you to a Capel Sink? White will be your Shirt.'

Sali Blaenpant gave Dan three sovereigns and a fat pig, and the pig he sold to Sam Warts, Castellybryn, and the money he got for it, and also the money he had had for the flesh of the pig which was sacrificed and the three sovereigns he put under the mattress of his bed.

On the eve of the Sabbath he said to the tale-bearers of the district: 'Jesus bach is inside me. Preach preaches will I on the first day in the void before the workshop of Lias Carpenter. Carpenter bach very handy was Jesus.'

The tale-bearers cried this to Bern-Davydd, whereof Bern-Davydd was uneasy, and he visited the houses of the men who had the oversight of the congregation.

'Fools you are,' he said to them. 'The cow Dan Groesfordd makes mischief in the Capel. Horrible, then. Abominable is the man. Don't be calm, old donkeys. Displeased will the Big Man be if this comes to pass. Your horses will rot and a plague of worms will eat your sheep. Lightning will burn your bellies and crops. And I, dear me, will be called to play the harp fach. What will you do without me?'

The men of the Big Seat took each other's counsel, and they conspired to do Dan hurt; they sent the lesser of the praying men to Groesfordd to stone him. Dan heard the noise of their footsteps and went softly into a place of concealment. Before the morning light he came abroad, and having eaten and put on him his black garments, he moved to the void place which is before the workshop of Lias Carpenter; and as he spoke Sali Blaenpant stepped downward from her cart and stood by him.

Some passed on their way to Sion, and were refreshed exceedingly with the music of his eloquence; they said: 'Preacher bach not very bad is Dan Shan.'

Dan preached for many Sabbaths, and the music of his eloquence gave religious delight to numerous persons; and every Sabbath Sali stayed by him. His name came to be greater than the name of Bern-Davydd, although Bern-Davydd accounted ill of him to God, and counselled God to blast his body. His ownings increased: he had a milching cow and a heifer, two pigs, three sheep, and many hens; and he hired a field besides the field which was marred with stones.

Bern-Davydd essayed to subdue him. He rehearsed wrathful words that he would relate to the assembly that gathered in the void place, but when he beheld all the people that Dan had stolen from Sion, his indignation was so great that he could not speak.

He turned away and walked to Capel Sion, and he said to the congregation: 'Foul old blacks are you to allow the mule to be more than the Big Man's son.'

A certain high man in the Big Seat ceased chewing his beard, and said: 'Wo, now, Religious Respected, not right that he speaks so of us, his children bach.'

'Dear me to goodness,' answered Bern-Davydd, 'go off, then, and pelt the male ram with your fists.'

The certain high man said: 'Good, too, that will be. How now if the young youths will do this for the Big Man's son? Take in your hands knobby batons.'

'Close your eyes, young youths, and the Big Man will say sayings in my ear,' said Bern-Davydd. In a little time he said: 'Like this the Large Judge: "Bern bach, array you the youths of Sion and send them out to whallop the frog Dan Groesfordd."'

Nine sons of Sion took Dan down from his bed, and they carried him to the pond which is in the close of Penparc, and they placed him on the brim of the mess, crying: 'Go inside, the man. Why for you do not go, I shouldn't be surprised!'

Because Dan hesitated, they urged him with the prongs of

hay forks, and when he came out of the messy water they took his clothes from his body and drove him home; at the gate of the close three of the young youths raised him from the ground and carried him into the house, and as they put him on his bed, they beheld that Sali Blaenpant and Shan were there also.

Now Bern-Davydd had seen from a secret place all this which was done to Dan, and it was so that he waited the return of the young youths in the way of the gate of the Shepherd's Abode.

'Fair day, porkers bach,' he said. 'How was affairs?'

'Fair day,' answered the youths. 'How was he?'

Then one said: 'Sali Blaenpant lies with Dan.'

'Porkers awful!' said Bern-Davydd. 'Mad is the shift of your tongues.'

'Truth we speak, Respected,' said the one who had spoken. 'In bed she is with him.'

Bern-Davydd was anxious; he spoke to himself: 'The hog will grow strong on Sali's riches. Hap she will build for him Capel Sink, and rob Sion still more. Go will I and look him in the face.'

He came to Groesfordd. 'How you was, religious one?' he said to Dan.

'Mouth of your spirit?' Dan asked.

'Big is the little mistake I made about you. Great is my think for the son of Shan.'

'Glad am I to listen to such and such,' said Dan.

'Iss-iss, the man. Speak you the day bach of the wedding to me.'

'Well, now,' said Dan.

'Riches you will inherit, Dan bach nice. There's useful yellow sovereigns are.'

'The earth is the Big Man's, Bern-Davydd,' said Dan. 'Selling Blaenpant is Sali fach, and the old money, will not I keep him in trust for the Big Man?'

'Daniel Groesfordd, make you a small prayer with clapped eyes, and I will listen for the speeches from the White Jesus bach to bid you to Sion.'

At the finish of Dan's prayer, Bern-Davydd said: 'Amen, boy bach. Amen and Amen. The large Jesus says: "Give Dan Groesfordd an important corner in the Big Seat."'

About the time that Dan was installed in the Big Seat in Sion, Sali laboured, and she delivered a child before the time was ripe for its birth. Yet the woman was puffed up: as it was buried she cried out: 'A photograph of the Big Man was the infant bach. Was he not Dan's son?'

Bern-Davydd said to Dan: 'Boy, boy, awful is this you have done. Heavy must be your sacrifice unto Sion.'

'Religious Respected,' answered Dan, 'deal him well by me. A bitch is the female.'

'Say now your offer, Dan Groesfordd.'

'Little have I of white silver and red pence,' said Dan.

'Give you five yellow sovereigns in the collection plate on Sabbath Preacher,' said Bern-Davydd.

'Nice little Respected Bern-Davydd, make you his talk less mean.'

'Five hundred of pounds and half hundred you had for Blaenpant, for sure.'

'Iss, dear me.'

'Giving you are, Dan Groesfordd, to Him,' said Bern-Davydd. 'There will be joy in the Palace.'

'Biggish was the price the rascal lawyer cost,' said Dan. 'There's old snails lawyers are.'

'Important is your corner in the Big Seat, man.'

'Say him a large yellow sovereign,' said Dan. 'Act him religious.'

Bern-Davydd replied: 'Put you the five yellow sovereigns in a parcel of paper, and form the words on the outside: "This is for the beloved Ruler bach." Go off up to the mountain will I then and tell the Big Man that you fell by an old female.'

Dan obeyed Bern-Davydd, and he wept in the Seiet that women had caused him to meddle with them to his hurt, and he glorified God that his hand had been stayed from marrying Sali Blaenpant.

The next day he performed a second sacrifice: he brought

out of Groesfordd the bed in which he had slept and an hour before the sun went down he burnt it because of its sin; and Shan he sent away to the House of the Poor, which is in Castellybryn, and he made Sali return to the district of her people, which is Conwil.

Afterwards there was peace on all sides of Sion.

# The Word

According to the Word of Davydd Bern-Davydd, the Respected of Capel Sion, which is in the parish of Troedfawr, in the Shire of Cardigan:

My text, congregation fach, is in Luke, the seventh chapter and the second after the tenth verse: 'Now when He came nigh to the gate of the city, behold, there was a dead man carried out, the only son of his mother, and she was a widow: and much people of the city was with her.' The second after the tenth verse in the seventh chapter of Luke, people: 'Now when He came nigh to the gate of the city, behold, there was a dead man carried out, the only son of his mother, and she was a widow; and much people of the city was with her.'

Search deeply into the verse will I. Going about preaching was the White Jesus bach. A student He was at this time, collecting for His College, like the students that come here from College Carmarthen and College Bala. Grand was the sermon He had worded at Capernaum. There's big the collection was. Then He said: 'For sure me, go I will to Capel Moriah in Nain.'

Was not Nain, people bach, a big town? Things very pretty were in the town. There were Capels in every part, and the largest was Capel Moriah Dissenters. Moriah had two lofts, and in front of the lower loft there was a clock cuckoo; and nice the ornaments in the ceiling were now. And there's a splendid pulpit, higher than even the roof of the heathen old Church. Boys bach, never have you seen such a Book of

Words. The cover was of leather; not hard leather, but soft like Mishtress Bern-Davydd's Sabbath shoes. And he had clasps of brass, and at the beginning of him was written the names of all the Rulers of Moriah.

Between the Capel and the road, as we have in Sion, was the burial ground, which from end to end measured more than from Shop Rhys to the tree on which Dennis sinned. The place was so big that you could not see the other side. Larger than ten hayfields. And as full of graves as a Ianto's field is of thistles. Very careful you had to be not to walk on the graves. Fuller, indeed, five over twenty times than the burial ground of Capel Horeb in Morfa.

Natty were the stones over the graves. Come with me, little men, and peep at them we will. Here is one above a Ruler of the Pulpit. Photographs of angels at the end of the stone. And what a big angel bach on the head. What is he doing? Sounding he is, indeed to goodness, the Harp of Gold. What is the name of the hymn the angel bach is toning?

> Guide me, O Thou great Redeemer,
>    Pilgrim through this barren land;
> I am weak, but Thou art mighty,
>    Hold me with Thy powerful hand;
>      Bread of Heaven,
> Feed me now and evermore.

What is the Ruler's name, say you? A surprise. Read you on the stone again. 'Here sleeps Solomon, who reigned over Israel for twice twenty years.'

Dear me, here is a nice stone and costly. This is over the perished body surely of a nobleman. Who was he? Hap he had a shop draper or a walk milk. Great he was in the Big Seat. 'He died in the Big Man's arms,' is the writing. O persons, shall that much be said of you? When you hear the trumpet noising over your grave, will you say: 'I am ready, White Jesus bach?' Shall that be said of you Dai Lanlas, after the report that Eynon Daviss made about you? A dirty black you was, man, to jeer at Capel Sion.

Come, let us leave fulbert Lanlas and read the stones and heed the flowers glass on the mounds. There is the Mishtress Simeon: 'Be this her Memorial.' Here is the grave of the religious little widow who gave her mite. 'Let this be counted unto her for righteousness.' A grand sampler was the widow. She gave her mite. Nanss Penfordd, one yellow sovereign and half a crown you gave last year to Sion, though you get a large pension. Isaac Brongest, man, increase your sacrifice, or complain to the Big Preacher I must.

What is this? An open grave. What are the names on the stone at the side? 'Abram Shop Grocer, Nain.' Was Abram religious? Great was the wealth he left his widow Esther. Ask askings we shall of the old gravedigger. There he is – a tallish man and hairless and his trousers are loosened because of the heat of the sun. Occupation very good is making graves. Digging the houses which shelter us between here and the Palace. Very happy are affairs in the grave, people.

'Fair day, little man, how you was then?'

'Good am I, strangers; and fair day to you. Where shall I say you hail from?'

'Boys bach from Capel Sion,' we say. 'Proud is the graveyard.'

The gravedigger rests his chin on the end of the rod of his pickaxe and wipes the tobacco spittle from his chin. 'Iss, man, when this coffin is covered, there will be no more room. Has not the Capel taken the spacious field of Eben son of Joseph? Elegant will be the to-do at the first opening.'

'The hole is not very large,' we say. 'Be he for a maid now?'

'No – no, male. Though he is narrow, he is not for a maid.'

'As you speak. Mouth who is perished.'

'A young youth,' the old gravedigger says. 'The son of Esther the widow of Abram Shop Grocer.'

'Don't say. When is the funeral, male bach?'

'This day, boys Capel Sion. An hour after the dinner.'

The gravedigger takes out his old watch. 'One o'clock. Saint Shames will be praying in the house now. Tearful are Shames's prayers. And Luke will speak also.'

'Who is Shames and Luke?'

Astonished is the gravedigger. 'Dullish you are. Is not Shames the Ruler of Capel Moriah in Jerusalem? And Luke bach the Ruler of Capel Antioch? Tuneful and short and sweet preacher is Luke bach the Singer. Do you tarry here to listen to his sermon over the coffin in the Capel. Treat you will have.'

He goes down into the hole and makes the walls straight. Listen, blockheads. Is he not singing one of Hawen's hymns? Hymner very religious is Hawen. Now he comes up and examines his watch. 'Late is the funeral,' he says. He stands on the hedge, but he sees no men and women walking and letting tears in their Sabbath clothes. He cries to Daniel bach Lions who is the Keeper of the House of the Capel: 'Slow is the carcase in coming, Daniel, now.' Daniel answers: 'Iss, indeed, sent Abed have I to seek reasons.'

The afternoon grows and no funeral. The day dims. We will stay on, companions, for are we not to hear Luke bach the Singer saying a sermon? Iss, then, we will stop.

So we tarry, and ask more questions of the gravedigger. 'Was this a promising young youth – the son of Esther the Widow of Abram Shop Grocer?'

'Indeed iss. Home he was from College Jerusalem. Did he not drive out the Bad Man from the body of a servant woman who had spoken ill of a teacher in the College? Learned he was in the School of Sunday. What is the matter for the funeral not to come? Dear me, don't say that Esther the Widow of Abram has perished and will be put in the grave with her son! Maybe Shames has the spirit on him. Shames prays sometimes for a week without a stop.'

Go we will to meet the funeral. But here is Abed bach coming on the Tramping road. His belly shivers like the belly of Rhys Shop when he was found sinning with Anna in the storehouse, and his thick lips are gaped like the lips of the Schoolin when he desires Ellen Felin.

'Boys, boys,' he cries. 'Are you waiting to see the funeral?'

'Iss – iss, man,' we answer.

'Then there is no funeral to be,' he says. 'The son of Esther is not dead.'

'Well – well?' we ask.

'He is risen.'

'Don't murmur idly,' says the gravedigger.

'Truth sure this is,' replies Abed. 'Esau and Jacob and Matthew and Job were carrying the coffin from the house into the hearse when the Big Jesus passed. He said to Esther: "Why for you weep?" And Esther told Him how Abram was in the Palace of White Shirts and now that her son was gone also there was none to care after the Shop Grocer. The White Jesus bach called up to him Samuel Carpenter and commanded him to unscrew the coffin. The young youth was alive.'

'Goodness all,' says the old boy of a gravedigger. 'Will He stay long in the land?'

O males Capel Sion, much was the noise in Nain that day. Samuel took away the coffin and the screws. Shames did not pray. Luke bach the short and sweet Singer put his funeral sermon in the backhead pocket of his preacher's coat.

While the young youth was preparing to go into the Shop, Esther his mother said to him: 'Boy bach, do you remember perishing?'

He answered: 'No.'

'Do you remember Sam Carpenter measuring you for a coffin?'

'No.'

'Do you remember the White Shirt?'

'No.'

'Did you hear Jesus speaking to you?'

'Iss, iss. I heard Him in Eternity.'

Glad was Esther the widow woman. 'Don't you hasten away, people,' she said. 'Stay you, and I will brew tea and make pancakes.'

And do you know, O creatures, no night followed that day in Nain. Men and women went about and abroad, saying one to another of this miracle which had taken place in the house of Esther Shop Grocer. For the Big Man had raised His voice to the Chief Angel: 'Put another wick in the sun.'

# The Comforter

The Respected Davydd Bern-Davydd lay on his face at the grave of his wife Sara, and while he wept he spoke: 'Perished is your carcase, Mishtress fach. Three tens and three years we lived together. And what was you doing now, Sara fach? Playing the little Harp. Unhappy am I without you. Did I not show you how to serve the Big Husband? Great One, why for you drowned the candle that was in the Shepherd's Abode? In a haste you was, God bach: an hour or two and cross Avon Jordan would me and Sara together.'

The congregation witnessed Bern-Davydd's solemn acting, and they said that the man's grief was heavy; and as eight of the strongest men in Capel Sion lifted the coffin and lowered it into the grave, every one that was of age bemoaned in an audible voice: 'Having gone, indeed me, is the wife of our Respected.'

After the grave was filled with earth and a mound was fashioned over it, Bern-Davydd commanded the people to go into the Capel; and he stepped briskly at the head of them, and they followed him in the manner of those that walk in procession. When all were gathered in Sion, Bern-Davydd went up into his pulpit and asked God by what violent means he could end his life. Then Bern-Davydd answered God: 'All right you are, now, then, Big Man. So-so. Live you want me to keep your House respectable.'

It fortuned that on the fifth Sabbath after Sara's burial Tim Deinol – Deinol is on the slope that goes down into Morfa – and his daughter Becca came into the neighbourhood to ask about the welfare of Josi Llandwr; Josi wished to wed Becca because he coveted Tim's belongings. They were arrived early in the day; and Tim put his horse in the stable which is against the House of the Capel, and he made himself familiar to Ben and Jane, the keepers thereof. These are the words with which Tim Deinol greeted Ben and Jane:

'How you was, boys bach?'

'How you was?' Ben answered.

'Give you the mare fach a feed of hay, now,' said Tim.

Having done that task, Ben returned, and to him Tim said: 'Journeyed to Capel Sion are we to hear the Evangel. From Morfa are we come to weep to the tune of the Respected. A deacon am I in Capel Saron. Do I not own Deinol, a farm, people bach, of three twenties and ten acres?'

As soon as Tim ceased his saying, Ben talked to Jane:

'Don't you stand there, old female, like a snake. Boil water at once in a hurry for to make little cups of tea. Sit they down in the best end of the house and tarry they till the moment they enter the Capel. Distant is the way from Morfa.'

Jane served the strangers with tea and with the luxuries of the land: butter and white bread, sugar in lumps, and such cheese as shopkeepers sell; and she placed an apron over Becca's lap so that neither the tea nor the food, if any fell thereon, should soil Becca's black cashmere frock. Becca was neither young nor well-favoured, and her forehead was marked with a blotch which was of the colour of a red cabbage.

In the course of his eating and drinking, Tim observed:

'Jasto, now, cold are my feet.'

Jane knelt down on her knees and took off his shoes and gave him a stool on which to rest his feet.

Then Ben withdrew and stood in the way of Sion's gate, and to the congregation which passed he spoke:

'A rich man has come from Morfa to weep joy under the Respected.'

'Speak you his name to us, man,' the congregation urged. 'There's close you are.'

'His name is Tim and his farm is Deinol, and he has hundreds of acres of land, and water flows through every field, and the number of his servants is six. Wicked animals, why you wait? Go off away to your pews and be presentable.'

In the fulness of time Bern-Davydd came into the House of the Capel and after he had drunk of tea and eaten of bread and butter he viewed Tim and Becca at a wide space, and he came up to them, saying:

'Male and wife from where you are?'

Tim and Becca made such reverence as is due unto the Judge of Sion; and Tim also uncovered his head: 'A little old man am I to baldness. The wench is my daughter Becca.'

'Ho – ho,' said Bern-Davydd. 'Tidy is the old wench.'

'As he speaks, Religious Respected,' said Tim.

'In a nice White Shirt is my Mishtress,' said Bern-Davydd. 'There's hard is my sorrow. Ask you of the congregation.'

'Sounds of his weeping have we heard in Morfa,' said Tim.

Bern-Davydd sang: 'A grand woman was the Mishtress. She obeyed her husband and gave me two sons. The Big Man gives and the Big Man takes away. Blessed be the name of the Big Man.'

'Amen, indeed. Amen. Amen,' said Tim.

Bern-Davydd asked: 'Say you the enterprise you have here?'

'Come are we to hear him expound,' answered Tim.

'Dear me, iss. Too religious am I to spout about old business. Stop you, now, farms fach very nice in the land.'

'That he says. Speak him the farm at the head of the old School?'

'Think you of Penparc?'

'No, no. High is the heap of manure in the close of her.'

'Is she not Llandwr?'

'Iss, Llandwr. Farmer very strong is Josi Llandwr?' asked Tim.

'Indeed, so-so.'

'Listen you, Becca,' said Tim.

The woman said: 'Ears have I got. What for you think?

Beautiful are the Respected's words.'

'Explain in a whisper why you demand about Josi?' said Bern-Davydd.

'Not this way; not that way. Heard have I of the boy.'

'No odds, male bach.'

'Iss – iss; no – no,' said Tim. 'Bulky is the purse his mother left him.'

'The Psalmist bach says: "Every man is a liar."'

'Wisdom very neat,' said Tim.

'Read you, dear me, the Book of Words. Now what the Psalmist mean? Every man. Not every ruler. The Big Man's son am I.'

'One waggled his tongue to me in this way: "Bulky is Josi's purse,"' said Tim.

Bern-Davydd answered Tim: 'Purses cannot play the Harp. In the Abode is the Mishtress's purse, and the Mishtress is playing the Harp. Boys bach, weep will I now badly.'

In the middle of the day Tim and Becca supped broth at Llandwr, and Josi closed his beady eyes and said: 'Make words will I to the Large One.'

Tim did not regard Josi's prayer, at the finish of which he said: 'Amen now indeed to goodness. Closing is the day. Do you now display your riches.'

'Gladly would I do that for you,' replied Josi, 'but is not this the Sabbath: Jealous of His day is the Big Man. How speeched He about the breaking of him?'

'Religious your say,' said Tim. 'Many blessings has the Farmer given to you.'

'Large, indeed, Tim Deinol. If this was an old week-day show you I would my cattle and crops.'

'For sure, boy bach.'

'And I would say: "Lucky is the female I shall wed." Youngish too am I: no razor has yet touched the down on my little face. Open my mouth I will now about religion. The Temple of Solomon was very pretty.'

Tim considered with himself: 'Much was the gold inside.'

'Male bach, iss. Did not Queen Sheba give Solomon a lot?

Rich was Solomon, and Queen gave him above one hundred and a half of yellow sovereigns.'

'Prydderch in his *Explanations* says that half a hundred was the sum. I could not give Becca as much.'

'Sorry am I that I threw gravel at the window of your wench fach,' said Josi. 'Well – well, grand bit of sermon this morning, man.'

'How if Becca brings with her a sow?' said Tim. 'Queen Sheba gave Solomon no pigs.'

'Swine the little White Jesus called pigs. Some were possessed. Ach y fi!'

'The swine the Big Man spoke of,' said Tim, 'were not the pigs we know. Did He not speak in a parable?'

'Tim Deinol,' said Josi, 'wrangle you about the Word?' Josi looked up to God: 'What do you think, now, Big Man! Tim Deinol denies the Word. Is he not a iob?' Thus saying he put on him his coat and his hat, and he feigned to go away.

His manner alarmed Tim, who laughed as frightened persons are accustomed to do. Tim said: 'What is the matter with the boy bach? Swine are little pigs.'

'And gold Queen Sheba gave Solomon,' said Josi. 'Many sovereigns.'

'Iss – iss.'

'The religious man gives all to his children.'

'As you say,' said Tim. 'Leave you two will I now to say this and that.' Therewith he went out and looked into Josi's barn, and he cast his gaze in search of implements which are employed on the land, and he studied the cattle which were in the fields of Llandwr; and he turned into the house. He said to Josi: 'Wed you Becca fach. And all I have shall be yours.' Immediately after he had spoken, he walked to the doorway, and on the threshold he spoke: 'That's a handy machine separator you've got, Josi.'

'No, man, no old separator have I,' answered Josi. 'Very useless she is.'

'Save much cream she does,' said Tim, 'when you have many cows.'

'The wench of a servant skims my cream,' said Josi.

'Large is the labour, dear me. Well, farewell, then, Josi.'

Now at the moment that Tim and his daughter were going away, Josi said: 'Do not go in secret. Pass you do the Shepherd's Abode. Pained will Bern-Davydd's mind be if privily you off.'

Even as Josi had desired, Tim stopped his mare and shouted: 'Helo, here. Shall I say there are men in the Shepherd's Abode?'

'Come down, small people from Morfa,' said Bern-Davydd. 'Reasoning with the Big Man am I.'

They two entered the Abode.

'Crafty boy is Josi Llandwr,' said Tim.

'Mouth you wisely,' said the preacher. 'Base is the turk and miserable. Deceit is in his clay and his debts are as many as there are flowers in his land.'

'Solemn serious, man nice! Say him more again.'

'Low is the black. "Denounce you Josi Llandwr in Sion, now, Bern," said the Big Man to me. "God bach," I answered, "without passion am I, indeed. And weary with sorrow." The Big Man answered: "Bern, for why you did not complain then, man? Send a wife to you I will in a hurry. But remember that bad is the herring of Llandwr. Has he not his eye on Becca Deinol? His old feet splay like the mouth of an avon."'

'Thanks very great to you, religious Respected,' said Tim. 'We in Saron shall wail for a whole night for Mishtress Bern-Davydd.'

Tim and Becca stayed over the night at the Shepherd's Abode, and in the morning they arose, Tim saying: 'Large thanks, Respected. Off we go.'

'Young is the day, dear me,' answered Bern-Davydd. 'Wait you a time bach.'

So Tim and Becca remained until near twilight, and they rose again.

But Bern-Davydd said: 'Don't you leave me now, then. Gone to the Palace has the Mishtress. Tarry you with me until the morning.'

As the light of that day was darkening, Tim said: 'Walking am I for the horse.'

'A terrible one you was,' cried Bern-Davydd. 'Sit you down, you and the wench.' He turned his face away, and he brought forth Sara's petticoat and frock. Of these he said: 'Stoutish was the Mishtress. Take you off your affair, Becca fach, and clothe yourself.'

Becca put on herself Sara's frock and petticoat, and she laughed, saying: 'Well – well, a large woman I feel. How shall I say?'

Bern-Davydd replied: 'A miracle bach the Big Father performed on Sara Abram.' He laid Sara's Sabbath boots at Becca's feet, and he raised his voice: 'Sit you down, Becca Tim Deinol, and draw the boots on your feet.'

# An Offender in Sion

For her stubbornness to her brother-in-law Ianto, who had a name above many in Capel Sion, the Big Man lamed Rachel, widow Enoch Coed, in her legs, and he branded her body with the prongs of pitching forks, so that at the judging his preachers shall remember her wickedness.

On a day Rachel spoke up against her brother-in-law, Ianto.

'Woman fach,' Ianto answered her, 'not very good are affairs. Do we have enough faith in the Large Farmer?'

Rachel replied that her brother-in-law's words were becoming.

'Glad would I be to let you stay in the small place,' said Ianto. 'Fertile is the land and worth many yellow sovereigns. Is not money a load on my soul? But the land belongs to the Big Man.'

'Like a preach is your mouthing,' said Rachel. 'Grand for you to say in that way.'

'Has He not talked: "I am the landlord of the Palace of White Shirts and the earth"?'

Divining the meaning of Ianto's words, Rachel cried hastily: 'Old thief you are, for sure. At his perishing did not your father give Coed to Enoch?'

Ianto observed Rachel: 'There's colour, dear me, in your face.'

'Fulbert very black you are,' said the woman.

'Say fairly will I now,' Ianto remarked. He laid his hands on Rachel's shoulders, and he spoke flatteringly, and made false promises. He said this also: 'Tidy, look you here, you are in your blood. Softening I am. Come you into the lower end and talk matters will we.'

Rachel placed her trust carelessly in him; and it came to be that after Ianto had committed his sin he repented and he rebuked Rachel: 'Awful, serpent, is this you have done.'

Wherefore Rachel laughed, saying: 'A baban bach I shall get and the name of his father I shall noise in Sion.'

'Shut your throat, temptress Coed,' Ianto commanded in his anger. 'Tell tellings of you will I in the ears of the Big Man. Much will be my muster.'

'Be you nice now,' said Rachel, 'and let me abide in the place bach.'

Ianto lamented: 'Ten over twenty was the age of Enoch when the Big Man struck him for wedding a pig-wife from Shire Pembroke.'

At the side of his bed he reported to the Big Man: that a woman had sought to hurt him, that the woman was of a loose nature, that her hair was yellower than the flowers which marred his cornfields, that the middle of her body was pressed in a manner most abominable unto Sion. He told how that the twelve acres of Coed land were as a wilderness of gorse and heather, how that broken hedges divided the fields, and how that the walls of the cowhouse were crumbled. 'Wifeless old boy am I,' he said, 'and there's an unsullied one. Barren was Rachel to Enoch. Keep you her barren, little Big Man.'

In the morning he went to Coed. Rachel saw him when he was afar off, and she put on her a white apron and she puffed up her hair.

'How you was, female?' asked Ianto.

Rachel feigned pleasure. 'Put yourself in a chair,' she said.

'Here am I on small business.'

'Certain sure me,' replied Rachel. 'Close the door will I.'

'No-no, Rachel Enoch Coed. Heap of dung you are to flaunt your body before me.'

'Deal you evenly now with your maid,' Rachel pleaded. 'Sorry am I to know your message.'

'Sober, serious is my inside.'

'Wait you a time bach, and all right will the land be. For two years have I laboured alone. Since Dan winged.'

'Windy is your speeching. Weep do I as I gaze upon the soil. Account must I give to the Farmer in the Big Farm. Go you off.'

But Rachel would not depart; and Ianto took counsel and was instructed how to seize Coed and all that was in the land and on the land. To Hews Auctions, who is skilful in these things, he said: 'Come you up, Hews bach, and make a writing of everything Rachel has. Charge nothing to your memory. Say you nothing. An old Pembroke pig is the wench. This is a whisper between us.'

Before Rachel was aroused, Hews was counting her belongings. When he had performed a little of his task, Rachel came to him and proved him, and after she had received his answers, she ran to Ianto's house; and she pursued her brother-in-law to the door of the lower end; and she screamed as a woman in childbirth.

'Rachel, now, indeed to goodness,' Ianto cried from within, 'still your tongue. Did not my religious father rest here in his White Shirt?'

Rachel would not be soothed.

In a great fear, Ianto stepped through the way of the window. Rachel heard his going, whereat she followed him into the close.

'Don't you be savage, little woman,' Ianto said. 'Turn your mind. Speak civil will I this one minute.'

'Son of hell on fire, why sent you Hews to spy my ownings?'

'Harsh you are. Boy pretty good is Hews. How says the Book of Advices: "Judge that you are not judged"? Iss, indeed, you, Rachel fach. You. Not me. Not Hews. You.'

'Tell him out.'

'No sense is in your spite. My arm is spread not against you. No, drop dead and blind. The lawyer rascal has done this.'

'You fondled me,' Rachel shouted. 'And am I not large? Stallion of a frisky frog you are.'

These sayings distressed Ianto, for he did not know whose ears received them. 'Jesabel,' he said lowly, 'shut your chin, or kick your belly will I.'

'Why then send me off?'

'Disquiet you are. The last Sabbath the Respected said: "Don't be greedy after old treasures, people bach."'

Ianto knelt and closed his eyes, and he prayed in behalf of Rachel's sins; and as he prayed Rachel threw a spade at him, and the spade cut into his flesh.

Thereafter Ianto hoarded his vengeance; and at his ordering Hews Auctions came to sell all that was in and about Coed. Rachel was strifeful and stayed in the house, and she cried at a window: 'I'll slay you, Hews bach.'

Hews was attended by the people, some of whom mimicked his halting footsteps. One said: 'Afraid you are of a hoyden.'

Rachel cast a stone. It struck Hews; the man fell, rose again, and escaped swiftly.

'Boys, boys, is she stronger than Sion?' Ianto asked the assembly. 'The little Big Man is on our side.'

The people strengthened their force; and many lifted their voices; 'Why for you not come out, whelp of an ass'; and they broke down the door. Beyond the threshold they beheld Rachel with a gun at her shoulder. They turned upon one another speedily, and each hid himself and none returned. All knew that Rachel had stored much violence in her bosom.

Ianto pondered: and he drove into one of Rachel's fields three yearling calves. Presently he arrived to view them, and, lo, one was missing.

'Hai, now,' he cried. 'Where is my calf bach?'

'Am I your shepherd?' Rachel answered.

'There's a cost are calves.'

'I killed your calf.'

Looking upwards, Ianto rebuked the Big Man: 'What for you say to this? Put my calf I did in your keeping. Higher prices was she than a sheep.' He roared his concern so loudly that his sound was heard beyond three fields.

Rachel would not cease her mischief. By day she guarded her house and by night she passed stealthily into her brother-in-law's land and maimed the cattle therein. It was so that Ianto watched for her comings, and at the dawn of a morning he came upon her; wherefore the woman, having knowledge of her danger, hasted into his barnyard and covered herself with straw. Ianto made a show of seeking her, but he did not go away from the barnyard. He summoned to him his manservant and his maidservant, to whom he said: 'Untidy is the yard. Clear the old straw we will into the stable. Get you pitchforks.'

Then they three drove their pitchforks into the straw.

# A Widow Woman

The Respected Davydd Bern-Davydd spoke in this sort to the people who were assembled at the Meeting for Prayer: 'Well-well, know you all the order of the service. Grand prayers pray last. Boys ordinary pray middle, and bad prayers pray first. Boys bach just beginning also come first. Now, then, after I've read a bit from the Book of Speeches and you've sung the hymn I call out, Josi Mali will report.'

Bern-Davydd ceased his reading, and while the congregation sang, Josi placed his arms on the sill which is in front of pews and laid his head thereon.

'Josi Mali, man, come to the Big Seat and mouth what you think,' said Bern-Davydd.

Josi's mother Mali touched her son, whispering this counsel: 'Put to shame the last prayer, indeed now, Josi.'

By and by Josi lifted his head and stood on his feet. This is what he said: 'Asking was I if I was religious enough to spout in the company of the Respected.'

'Out of the necks of young youths we hear pieces that are very sensible,' said Bern-Davydd. 'Come you, Josi Mali, to the saintly Big Seat.'

As Josi moved out of the pew, his thick lips fallen apart and his high cheek bones scarlet, his mother said: 'Keep your eyes clapped very close, or hap the prayers will shout that you spoke from a hidden book like an old parson.'

So Josi, who in the fields and on his bed had exercised prayer in the manner that one exercises singing, uttered his first petition in Capel Sion. He told the Big Man to pardon the weakness of his words, because the trousers of manhood had not been long upon him; he named those who entered the Tavern and those who are bread which had been swollen by barm; he congratulated God that Bern-Davydd ruled over Sion.

At what time he was done, Bern-Davydd cried out: 'Amen. Solemn, dear me, amen. Piece quite tidy of prayer'; and the men of the Big Seat cried: 'Piece quite tidy of prayer.'

The quality of Josi's prayers gave much pleasure in Sion, and it was noised abroad even in Morfa, from whence a man journeyed, saying: 'Break your hire with your master and be a servant in my farm. Wanting a prayer very bad do we in Capel Salem.' Josi immediately asked leave of God to tell Bern-Davydd that which the man from Morfa had said. God gave him leave, wherefore Bern-Davydd, whose spirit waxed hot, answered: 'Boy, boy, why for did you not kick the she cat on the backhead?'

Then Josi said to his mother Mali: 'A preacher will I be. Go will I at the finish of my servant term to the school for Grammar in Castellybryn.'

'Glad am I to hear you talk,' said Mali. 'Serious pity that my belongings are so few.'

'Small is your knowledge of the Speeches,' Josi rebuked his mother. 'How go they: "Sell all that you have?" Iss-iss, all, mam fach.'

Now Mali lived in Pencoch, which is in the valley about midway between Shop Rhys and the Schoolhouse, and she rented nearly nine acres of the land which is on the hill above Sion. Beyond the furnishings of her two-roomed house, she owned three cows, a heifer, two pigs, and fowls. She fattened her pigs and sold them, and she sold also her heifer; and Josi went to the School of Grammar. Mali laboured hard on the land, and she got therefrom all that there was to be got; and whatever that she earned she hid in a hole in the ground. "Handy is little money,' she murmured, 'to pay for lodgings and clothes preacher, and the old scamps of boys who teach him.' She lived on potatoes and buttermilk, and she dressed her land all the time. People came to remark of her: 'There's no difference between Mali Pencoch and the mess in her cowhouse.'

Days, weeks, and months moved slowly; and years sped. Josi passed from the School of Grammar to College Carmarthen, and Mali gave him all the money that she had, and prayed thus: 'Big Man bach, terrible would affairs be if I perished before the boy was all right. Let you me keep my strength that Josi becomes as large as Bern-Davydd. Amen.'

Even so. Josi had a name among Students' College, and even among ordained rulers of pulpits; and Mali went about her duties joyful and glad; it was as if the Kingdom of the Palace of White Shirts was within her. While at her labour she mumbled praises to the Big Man for His goodness, until an awful thought came to her: 'Insulting am I to the Large One bach. Only preachers are holy enough to stand in their pray. Not stop must I now; go on my knees will I in the dark.'

She did not kneel on her knees for the stiffness that was in her limbs.

Her joy was increased exceedingly when Josi was called to minister unto Capel Beulah in Carmarthen, and she boasted: 'Bigger than Sion is Moriah and of lofts has not the Temple two?'

'Idle is your babbling,' one admonished her. 'Does a calf feed his mother?'

Josi heard the call. His name grew; men and women spoke his sayings one to another, and Beulah could not contain all the people who would hear his word; and he wrote a letter to his mother: 'God has given me to wed Mary Ann, the daughter of Daniel Shop Guildhall. Kill you a pig and salt him and send to me the meat.'

All that Josi asked Mali gave, and more; she did not abate in any of her toil for five years, when a disease laid hold on Josi and he died. Mali cleaned her face and her hands in the Big Pistil from which you draw drinking water, and she brought forth her black garments and put them on her; and because of her age she could not weep. The day before that her son was to be buried, she went to the house of her neighbour Sara Eye Glass, and to her she said: 'Wench nice, perished is Josi and off away am I. Console his widow fach I must. Tell you me that you will milk my cow.'

Sara turned her seeing eye upon Mali. 'An old woman very mad you are to go two nines of miles.'

'Milk you my cow,' said Mali. 'And milk you her dry. Butter from me the widow fach shall have. And give ladlings of the hogshead to my pigs and scatter food for my hens.'

She tore a baston from a tree, trimmed it and blackened it with blacking, and at noon she set forth to the house of her daughter-in-law; and she carried in a basket butter, two dead fowls, potatoes, carrots, and a white-hearted cabbage, and she came to Josi's house in the darkness which is in the morning, and it was so that she rested on the threshold; and in the bright light Mary Ann opened the door, and was astonished. 'Mam-in-law,' she said, 'there's nasty for you to come like this. Speak what you want. Sitting there is not respectable. You are like an old woman from the country.'

'Come am I to sorrow,' answered Mali. 'Boy all grand was Josi bach. Look at him now will I.'

'Talking no sense you are,' said Mary Ann. 'Why you do not see that the house is full of muster? Will there not be many Respecteds at the funeral?'

'Much preaching shall I say?'

'Indeed, iss. But haste about now and help to prepare food to eat. Slow you are, female.'

Presently mourners came to the house, and when each had walked up and gazed upon the features of the dead, and when the singers had sung and the Respecteds had spoken, and while a carpenter turned screws into the coffin, Mary Ann said to Mali: 'Clear you the dishes now, and cut bread and spread butter for those who will return after the funeral. After all have been served go you home to Pencoch.' She drew a veil over her face and fell to weeping as she followed the six men who carried Josi's coffin to the hearse.

Having finished, Mali took her baston and her empty basket and began her journey. As she passed over Towy Street – the public way which is strewn with stones – she saw that many people were gathered at the gates of Beulah to witness Mary Ann's loud lamentations at Josi's grave.

Mali stayed a little time; then she went on, for the light was dimming. At the hour she reached Pencoch the mown hay was dry and the people were gathering it together. She cried outside the house of Sara Eye Glass: 'Large thanks, Sara fach. Home am I, and like pouring water were the tears. And there's preaching.' She milked her cows and fed her pigs and her fowls, and then she stepped up to her bed. The sounds of dawn aroused her. She said to herself: 'There's sluggish am I. Dear-dear, rise must I in a haste, for Mary Ann will need butter to feed the baban bach that Josi gave her.'

# Joseph's House

A woman named Madlen, who lived in Penlan – the crumbling mud walls of which are in a nook of the narrow lane that rises from the valley of Bern – was concerned about the future state of her son Joseph. Men who judged themselves worthy to counsel her gave her such counsels as these: 'Blower bellows for the smith,' 'Cobblar clox,' 'Booboo for crows.'

Madlen flattered her counsellors, albeit none spoke that which was pleasing unto her.

'Cobblar clox, ach y fy,' she cried to herself. 'Wan is the lad bach with decline. And unbecoming to his Nuncle Essec that he follows low tasks.'

Moreover, people, look you at John Lewis. Study his marble gravestone in the burial ground of Capel Sion: 'His name is John Newton-Lewis; Paris House, London, his address. From his big shop in Putney, Home they brought him by railway.' Genteel are shops for boys who are consumptive. Always dry are their coats and feet, and they have white cuffs on their wrists and chains on their waistcoats. Not blight nor disease nor frost can ruin their sellings. And every minute their fingers grabble in the purses of nobles.

So Madlen thought, and having acted in accordance with her design, she took her son to the other side of Avon Bern, that is to Capel Mount Moriah, over which Essec her husband's brother lorded; and him she addressed decorously, as one does address a ruler of the capel.

'Your help I seek,' she said.

'Poor is the reward of the Big Preacher's son in this part,' Essec announced. 'A lot of atheists they are.'

'Not pleading I have not the rent am I,' said Madlen. 'How if I prentice Joseph to a shop draper. Has he any odds?'

'Proper that you seek,' replied Essec. 'Seekers we all are. Sit you. No room there is for Joseph now I am selling Penlan.'

'Like that is the plan of your head?' Madlen murmured, concealing her dread.

'Seven of pounds of rent is small. Sell at eighty I must.'

'Wait for Joseph to prosper. Buy then he will. Buy for your mam you will, Joseph?'

'Sorry I cannot change my think,' Essec declared.

'Hard is my lot; no male have I to ease my burden.'

'A weighty responsibility my brother put on me,' said Essec. '"Dying with old decline I am," the brother mouthed. "Fruitful is the soil. Watch Madlen keeps her fruitful." But I am generous. Eight shall be the rent. Are you not the wife of my flesh?'

After she had wiped away her tears, 'Be kind,' said Madlen, 'and wisdom it to Joseph.'

'The last evening in the seiet I commanded the congregation to give the Big Man's photograph a larger hire,' said Essec. 'A few of my proverbs I will now spout.' He spat his spittle and bundling his beard blew the residue of his nose therein; and he chanted: 'Remember Essec Pugh, whose right foot is tied into a club knot. Here's the club to kick sinners as my perished brother tried to kick the Bad Satan from the inside of his female Madlen with his club of his baston. Some preachers search over the Word. Some preachers search in the Word. But search under the Word does preacher Capel Moriah. What's the light I find? A stutterer was Moses. As the middle of a butter cask were the knees of Paul. A splotch like a red cabbage leaf was on the cheek of Solomon. By the signs shall the saints be known. "Preacher Club Foot, come forward to tell about Moriah," the Big Man will say. Mean scamps, remember Essec Pugh, for I shall remember you the Day of Rising.'

It came to be that on a morning in the last month of his thirteenth year Joseph was bidden to stand at the side of the cow which Madlen was milking and to give an ear to these commandments: 'The serpent is in the bottom of the glass. The hand on the tavern window is the hand of Satan. On the Sabbath eve get one penny for two ha'pennies for the plate collection. Put money in the handkerchief corner. Say to persons you are a nephew of Respected Essec Pugh and you will have credit. Pick the white sixpence from the floor and give her to the mishtir; she will have fallen from his pocket trowis.'

Then Joseph turned, and carrying his yellow tin box, he climbed into the craggy moorland path which takes you to the Tramping road. By the pump of Tavarn Ffos he rested until Shim Carrier came thereby; and while Shim's horse drank of barley water, Joseph stepped into the waggon; and at the end of the passage Shim showed him the business of getting a ticket and that of going into and coming down from a railway carriage.

In that manner did Joseph go to the drapery shop of Rees Jones in Carmarthen; and at the beginning he was instructed in the keeping and the selling of such wares as reels of cotton, needles, pins, bootlaces, mending wool, buttons, and such like – all those things which together are known as haberdashery. He marked how this and that were done, and in what sort to fashion his visage and frame his phrases to this or that woman. His oncoming was rapid. He could measure, cut, and wrap in a parcel twelve yards of brown or white calico quicker than any one in the shop, and he understood by rote the folds of linen tablecloths and bedsheets; and in the town this was said of him: 'Shopmen quite ordinary can sell what a customer wants; Pugh Rees Jones can sell what nobody wants.'

The first year passed happily, and the second year; and in the third Joseph was stirred to go forward.

'What use to stop here all the life?' he asked himself. 'Better to go off.'

## Joseph's House

He put his belongings in his box and went to Swansea.

'Very busy emporium I am in,' were the words he sent to Madlen. 'And the wage is twenty pounds.'

Madlen rejoiced at her labour and sang: 'Ten acres of land, and a cowhouse with three stalls and a stall for the new calf, and a pigstye, and a house for my bones and a barn for my hay and straw, and a loft for my hens: why should men pray for more?' She ambled to Moriah, diverting passers-by with boastful tales of Joseph, and loosened her imaginings to the Respected.

'Pounds without number he is earning,' she cried. 'Rich he'll be. Swells are youths shop.'

'Gifts from the tip of my tongue fell on him,' said Essec. 'Religious were my gifts.'

'Iss, indeed, the brother of the male husband.'

'Now you can afford nine of pounds for the place. Rich he is and richer he will be. Pounds without number he has.'

Madlen made a record of Essec's scheme for Joseph; and she said also: 'Proud I'll be to shout that my son bach bought Penlan.'

'Setting aside money am I,' Joseph speedily answered.

Again ambition aroused him. 'Footling is he that is content with Zwanssee. Next half-holiday skurshon I'll crib in Cardiff.'

Joseph gained his desire, and the chronicle of his doings he sent to his mother. 'Twenty-five, living-in, and spiffs on remnants are the wages,' he said. 'In the flannelette department I am and I have not been fined once. Lots of English I hear, and we call ladies madam that the wedded nor the unwedded are insulted. Boys harmless are the eight that sleep by me. Examine Nuncle of the price of Penlan.'

'I will wag my tongue craftily and slowly,' Madlen vowed as she crossed her brother-in-law's threshold.

'In Shire Pembroke land is cheap,' she said darkly.

'Look you for a farm there,' said Essec. 'Pelted with offers am I for Penlan. Ninety I shall have. Poverty makes me sell very soon.'

'As he says.'

'Pretty tight is Joseph not to buy her. No care has he for his mam.'

'Stiffish are affairs with him, poor dab.'

Madlen reported to Joseph that which Essec had said, and she added: 'Awful to leave the land of your father. And auction the cows. Even the red cow that is a champion for milk. Where shall I go? The House of the Poor. Horrid that your mam must go to the House of the Poor.'

Joseph sat on his bed, writing: 'Taken ten pounds from the post I have which leaves three shillings. Give Nuncle the ten as earnest of my intention.'

Nine years after that day on which he had gone to Carmarthen Joseph said in his heart: 'London shops for experience'; and he caused a frock coat to be sewn together, and he bought a silk hat and an umbrella, and at the spring cribbing he walked into a shop in the West End of London, asking: 'Can I see the engager, pleaze?' The engager came to him and Joseph spoke out: 'I have all-round experience. Flannelettes three years in Niclass, Cardiff, and left on my own accord. Kept the coloured dresses in Tomos, Zwanssee. And served through. Apprentized in Reez Jones Carmarthen for three years. Refs egzellent. Good ztok-keeper and appearance.'

'Start at nine o'clock Monday morning,' the engager replied. 'Thirty pounds a year and spiffs; to live in. You'll be in the laces.'

'Fashionable this shop is,' Joseph wrote to Madlen, 'and I have to be smart and wear a coat like the preachers, and mustn't take more than three zwap lines per day or you have the sack. Two white shirts per week; and the dresses of the showroom young ladies are a treat. Five pounds enclosed for Nuncle.'

'Believe your mam,' Madlen answered: 'don't throw gravel at the windows of the old English unless they have the fortunes.'

In his zeal for his mother's welfare Joseph was heedless of himself, eating little of the poor food that was served him, clothing his body niggardly, and seldom frequenting public bath-houses; his mind spanned his purpose, choosing the fields he would join to Penlan, counting the number of cattle that would graze on the land, planning the slate-tiled house which he would set up.

'Twenty pounds more must I have,' he moaned, "for the blaguard Nuncle.'

Every day thereafter he stole a little money from his employers and every night he made peace with God: 'Only twenty-five is the wage, and spiffs don't count because of the fines. Don't you let me be found out, Big Man bach. Will you strike mam into her grave? And disgrace Respected Essec Pugh Capel Moriah?'

He did not abate his energies howsoever hard his disease was wasting and destroying him. The men who lodged in his bedroom grew angry with him. 'How can we sleep with your dam coughing?' they cried. 'Why don't you invest in a second-hand coffin?'

Feared that the women whom he served would complain that the poison of his sickness was tainting them and that he would be sent away, Joseph increased his pilferings; where he had stolen a shilling he now stole two shillings; and when he got five pounds above the sum he needed, he heaved a deep sigh and said: 'Thank you for your favour, God bach. I will now go home to heal myself.'

Madlen took the money to Essec coming back heavy with grief.

'Hoo-hoo,' she whined, 'the ninety has bought only the land. Selling the houses is Essec.'

'Wrong there is,' said Joseph. 'Probe deeply we must.'

From their puzzlings Madlen said: 'What will you do?'

'Go and charge swindler Moriah.'

'Meddle not with him. Strong he is with the Lord.'

'Teach him will I to pocket my honest wealth.'

Because of his weakness, Joseph did not go to Moriah; today he said: 'I will tomorrow,' and tomorrow he said: 'Certain enough I'll go tomorrow.'

In the twilight of an afternoon he and Madlen sat down,

gazing about, and speaking scantily; and the same thought was with each of them, and this was the thought: 'A tearful prayer will remove the Big Man from his judgment, but nothing will remove Essec from his purpose.'

'Mam fach,' said Joseph, 'how will things be with you?'

'Sorrow not, soul nice,' Madlen entreated her son. 'Couple of weeks very short have I to live.'

'As an hour is my space. Who will stand up for you?'

'Hish, now. Hish-hish, my little heart.'

Madlen sighed; and at the door she made a great clatter, and the sound of the clatter was less than the sound of her wailing.

'Mam! Mam!' Joseph shouted. 'Don't you scream. Hap you will soften Nuncle's heart if you say to him that my funeral is close.'

Madlen put a mourning gown over her petticoats and a mourning bodice over her shawls, and she tarried in a field as long as it would take her to have travelled to Moriah; and in the heat of the sun she returned, laughing.

'Mistake, mistake,' she cried. 'The houses are ours. No understanding was in me. Cross was your Nuncle. "Terrible if Joseph is bad with me," he said. Man religious and tidy is Essec.' Then she prayed that Joseph would die before her fault was found out.

Joseph did not know what to do for his joy. 'Well-well, there's better I am already,' he said. He walked over the land and coveted the land of his neighbours. 'Dwell here for ever I shall,' he cried to Madlen. 'A grand house I'll build – almost as grand as the houses of preachers.'

In the fifth night he died, and before she began to weep, Madlen lifted her voice: 'There's silly, dear people, to covet houses! Only a smallish bit of house we want.'

# *Earthbred*

Because he was diseased with a consumption, Evan Roberts in his thirtieth year left over being a drapery assistant and had himself hired as a milk roundsman.

A few weeks thereafter he said to Mary, the woman whom he had promised to wed: 'How now if I had a milk-shop?'

Mary encouraged him, and searched for that which he desired; and it came to be that on a Thursday afternoon they two met at the mouth of Worship Street – the narrow lane that is at the going into Richmond.

'Stand here, Marri,' Evan ordered. 'Go in will I and have words with the owner. Hap I shall uncover his tricks.'

'Very well you are,' said Mary. 'Don't over-waggle your tongue. Address him in hidden phrases.'

Evan entered the shop, and as there was no one therein he made an account of the tea packets and flour bags which were on the shelves. Presently a small, fat woman stood beyond the counter. Evan addressed her in English: 'Are you Welsh?'

'That's what people say,' the woman answered.

'Glad am I to hear you,' Evan returned in Welsh. 'Tell me how you was.'

'A Cymro bach I see,' the woman cried. 'How was you?'

'Peeped did I on your name on the sign. Shall I say you are Mistress Jinkins?'

'Iss, indeed, man.'

'What about affairs these close days?'

'Busy we are. Why for you ask? Trade you do in milk?'

'Blurt did I for nothing,' Evan replied.

'No odds, little man. Ach y fy, jealous other milkmen are of us. There's nasty some people are.'

'Natty shop you have. Little shop and big traffic, Mistress Jinkins?'

'Quick you are.'

'Know you Tom Mathias Tabernacle Street?' Evan inquired.

'Seen him have I in the big meetings at Capel King's Cross.'

'Getting on he is, for certain sure. Hundreds of pints he sells. And groceries.'

'Pwf,' Mrs Jenkins sneered. 'Fulbert you are to believe him. A liar without shame is Twm. And a cheat. Bad sampler he is of the Welsh.'

'Speak I do as I hear. More thriving is your concern.'

'No boast is in me. But don't we do thirty gallons?'

Evan summoned up surprise into his face, and joy. 'Dear me to goodness,' he exclaimed. 'Take something must I now. Sell you me an egg.'

Evan shook the egg at his ear. 'She is good,' he remarked.

'Weakish is the male,' observed Mrs Jenkins. 'Much trouble he has in his inside.'

'Poor bach,' replied Evan. 'Well-well. Fair night for today.'

'Why for you are in a hurry?'

'Woman fach, for what you do not know that I abide in Wandsworth and the clock is late?'

Mrs Jenkins laughed. 'Boy pretty sly you are. Come you to Richmond to buy one egg?'

Evan coughed and spat upon the ground, and while he cleaned away his spittle with a foot he said: 'Courting business have I on the Thursdays. The wench is in a shop draper.'

'How shall I mouth where she is? With Wright?'

'In shop Breach she is.' He spoke this in English: 'So long.'

In that language also did Mrs Jenkins answer him. 'Now we shan't be long.'

Narrowing his eyes and crooking his knees, Evan stood

before Mary. 'Like to find out more would I,' he said. 'Guess did the old female that I had seen the adfertissment.'

'Blockhead you are to bare your mind,' Mary admonished him.

'Why for you call me blockhead when there's no blockhead to be?'

'Sorry am I, dear heart. But do you hurry to marry me. You know that things are so and so. The month has shown nothing.'

'Shut your head, or I'll change my think altogether.'

The next week Evan called at the dairy shop again.

'How was the people?' he cried on the threshold.

Mrs Jenkins opened the window which was at the back of her, and called out: 'The boy from Wales is here, Dai.'

Stooping as he moved through the way of the door, Dai greeted Evan civilly: 'How was you this day?'

'Quite grand,' Evan answered.

'What capel do you go?'

'Walham Green, dear man.'

'Good preach there was by the Respected Eynon Daviss the last Sabbath morning, shall I ask? Eloquent is Eynon.'

'In the night do I go.'

'Solemn serious, go you ought in the mornings.'

'Proper is your saying,' Evan agreed. 'Perform I would if I could.'

'Biggish is your round, perhaps?' said Dai.

'Iss–iss. No–no.' Evan was confused.

'Don't be afraid of your work. Crafty is your manner.'

Evan had not anything to say.

'Fortune there is in milk,' said Dai. 'Study you the size of her. Little she is. Heavy will be my loss. The rent is only fifteen bob a week. And thirty gallons and more do I do. Broke is my health,' and Dai laid the palms of his hands on his belly and groaned.

'Here he is to visit his wench,' said Mrs Jenkins.

'You're not married now just?' asked Dai.

'Better in his pockets trousers is a male for a woman,' said Mrs Jenkins.

'Comforting in your pockets trousers is a woman,' Dai cried.

'Clap your throat,' said Mrs Jenkins. 'Redness you bring to my skin.'

Evan retired and considered.

'Tempting is the business,' he told Mary. 'Fancy do I to know more of her. Come must I still once yet.'

'Be not slothful,' Mary pleaded. 'Already I feel pains, and quickly the months pass.'

Then Evan charged her to watch over the shop, and to take a count of the people who went into it. So Mary walked in the street. Mrs Jenkins saw her and imagined her purpose, and after she had proved her, she and Dai formed a plot whereby many little children and young youths and girls came into the shop. Mary numbered every one, but the number that she gave Evan was three times higher than the proper number. The man was pleased, and he spoke out to Dai. 'Tell me the price of the shop,' he said.

'Improved has the health,' replied Dai. 'And not selling I don't think am I.'

'Pity that is. Great offer I have.'

'Smother your cry. Taken a shop too have I in Petersham. Rachel will look after this.'

Mrs Jenkins spoke to her husband with a low voice: 'Witless you are. Let him speak figures.'

'As you want if you like then,' said Dai.

'A puzzle you demand this one minute,' Evan murmured. 'Thirty pounds would –'

'Light is your head,' Dai cried. 'More than thirty gallons and a pram. Eighty I want for the shop and stock.'

'I stop,' Evan pronounced. 'Thirty-five can I give. No more and no less.'

'Cute bargainer you are. Generous am I to give back five pounds for luck cash on spot. Much besides is my counter trade.'

'Bring me papers for my eyes to see,' said Evan.

Mrs Jenkins rebuked Evan: 'Hoity-toity! Not Welsh you are. Old English boy.'

'Tut–tut, Rachel fach,' said Dai. 'Right you are, and right and wrong is Evan Roberts. Books I should have. Trust I give and trust I take. I have no guile.'

'How answer you to thirty-seven?' asked Evan. 'No more we've got, drop dead and blind.'

He went away and related all to Mary.

'Lose the shop you will,' Mary warned him. 'And that's remorseful you'll be.'

'Like this and that is the feeling,' said Evan.

'Go to him,' Mary counselled, 'and say you will pay forty-five.'

'No–no, foolish that is.'

They two conferred with each other, and Mary gave to Evan all her money, which was almost twenty pounds; and Evan said to Dai: 'I am not doubtful –'

'Speak what is in you,' Dai urged quickly.

'Test your shop will I for eight weeks as manager. I give you twenty down as earnest and twenty-five at the finish of the weeks if I buy her.'

Dai and Rachel weighed that which Evan had proposed. The woman said: 'A lawyer will do this'; the man said: 'Splendid is the bargain and costly and thievish are old lawyers.'

In this sort Dai answered Evan: 'Do as you say. But I shall not give money for your work. Act you honestly by me. Did not mam carry me next my brother, who is a big preacher? Lend you will I a bed, and a dish or two and a plate, and a knife to eat food.'

At this Mary's joy was abounding. 'Put you up the banns,' she said.

'Lots of days there is. Wait until I've bought the place.'

Mary tightened her inner garments and loosened her outer garments, and every evening she came to the shop to prepare food for Evan, to make his bed, and to minister to him as a woman.

Now the daily custom at the shop was twelve gallons of milk, and the tea packets and flour bags which were on shelves were empty. Evan's anger was awful. He upbraided Mary, and he prayed to be shown how to worst Dai. His prayer was respected: at the end of the second week he gave Dai two pounds more than he had given him the week before.

'Brisk is trade,' said Dai.

'I took into stock flour, tea, and four tins of job biscuits,' replied Evan. 'Am I not your servant?'

'Well done, good and faithful servant.'

It was so that Evan bought more than he would sell, and each week he held a little money by fraud; and matches also and bundles of firewood and soap did he buy in Dai's name.

In the middle of the eighth week Dai came down to the shop.

'How goes it?' he asked in English.

'Fine, man. Fine.' Changing his language, Evan said: 'Keep her will I, and give you the money as I pledged. Take you the sum and sign you the paper bach.'

Having acted accordingly, Dai cast his gaze on the shelves and on the floor, and he walked about judging aloud the value of what he saw: 'Tea, three-pound-ten; biscuits, four-six; flour, forty-five; firewood, five shillings; matches, one-ten; soap, one pound. Bring you these to Petersham. Put you them with the bed and the dishes I kindly lent you.'

'For sure me, fulfil my pledge will I,' Evan said.

He assembled Dai's belongings and placed them in a cart which he had borrowed; and on the back of the cart he hung a Chinese lantern which had in it a lighted candle. When he arrived at Dai's house, he cried: 'Here is your ownings. Unload you them.'

Dai examined the inside of the cart. 'Mistake there is, Evan. Where's the stock?'

'Did I not pay you for your stock and shop? Forgetful you are.'

Dai's wrath was such that neither could he blaspheme God nor invoke His help. Removing the slabber which was gathered in his beard and at his mouth, he shouted: 'Put police on you will I.'

'Away must I now,' said Evan. 'Come, take your bed.'

'Not touch anything will I. Rachel witness his roguery. Steal he does from the religious.'

Evan drove off, and presently he became uneasy of the evil that might befall him were Dai and Rachel to lay their hands on him; he led his horse into the unfamiliar and hard and steep road which goes up to the Star and Garter, and which therefrom falls into Richmond town. At what time he was at the top he heard the sound of Dai and Rachel running to him, each screaming upon him to stop. Rachel seized the bridle of the horse, and Dai tried to climb over the back of the cart. Evan bent forward and beat the woman with his whip, and she leaped aside. But Dai did not release his clutch, and because the lantern swayed before his face he flung it into the cart.

Evan did not hear any more voices, and misdeeming that he had got the better of his enemies, he turned, and, lo, the bed was in a yellow flame. He strengthened his legs and stretched out his thin upper lip, and pulled at the reins, saying: 'Wo, now.' But the animal thrust up its head and on a sudden galloped downwards. At the railing which divides two roads it was hindered, and Evan was thrown upon the ground. Men came forward to lift him, and he was dead.

## According to the Pattern

On the eve of a Communion Sunday Simon Idiot espied Dull Anna washing her feet in the spume on the shore; he came out of his hiding-place and spoke jestingly to Anna and enticed her into Blind Cave, where he had sport with her. In the ninth year of her child, whom she had called Abel, Anna stretched out her tongue at the schoolmaser and took her son to the man who farmed Deinol.

'Brought have I your scarecrow,' she said. 'Give you to me the brown pennies that you will pay for him.'

From dawn to sunset Abel stood on a hedge, waving his arms, shouting, and mimicking the sound of gunning. Weary of his work he vowed a vow that he would not keep at it. He walked to Morfa and into his mother's cottage; his mother listened to him, then she took a stick and beat him until he could not rest nor move with ease.

'Break him in like a frisky colt, little man bach,' said Anna to the farmer. 'Know you he is the son of Satan. Have I not told how the Bad Man came to me in my sound sleep and was naughty with me?'

But the farmer had compassion on Abel and dealt with him kindly, and when Abel married he let him live in Tybach – the mud-walled, straw-thatched, two-roomed house which is midway on the hill that goes down from Synod Inn into Morfa – and he let him farm six acres of land.

The young man and his bride so laboured that the people thereabout were confounded; they stirred earlier and lay down later than any honest folk; and they took more eggs and tubs of butter to market than even Deinol, and their pigs fattened wondrously quick.

Twelve years did they live thus wise. For the woman these were years of toil and child-bearing; after she had borne seven daughters, her sap husked and dried up.

Now the spell of Abel's mourning was one of ill-fortune for Deinol, the master of which was grown careless: hay rotted before it was gathered and corn before it was reaped, potatoes were smitten by a blight, a disease fell upon two cart-horses, and a heifer was drowned in the sea. Then the farmer felt embittered, and by day and night he drank himself drunk in the inns of Morfa.

Because he wanted Deinol, Abel brightened himself up: he wore whipcord leggings over his short legs, and a preacher's coat over his long trunk, a white and red patterned celluloid collar about his neck, and a bowler hat on the back of his head; and his side-whiskers were trimmed in the shape of a spade. He had joy of many widows and spinsters, to each of whom he said: 'There's a grief-livener you are,' and all of whom he gave over on hearing of the widow of Drefach. Her he married, and with the money he got with her, and the money he borrowed, he bought Deinol. Soon he was freed from the hands of his lender. He had eight horses and twelve cows, and he had oxen and heifers, and pigs and hens, and he had twenty-five sheep grazing on his moorland. As his birth and poverty had caused him to be scorned, so now his gains caused him to be respected. The preacher of Capel Dissenters in Morfa saluted him on the Tramping road and in shop, and brought him down from the gallery to the Big Seat. Even if Abel had land, money, and honour, his vessel of contentment was not filled until his wife went into her deathbed and gave him a son.

'Indeed me,' he cried, 'Benshamin his name shall be. The Large Maker gives and a One He is for taking away.'

He composed a prayer of thankfulness and of sorrow; and

this prayer he recited to the congregation which gathered at the graveside of the woman from Drefach.

Benshamin grew up in the way of Capel Dissenters. He slept with his father and ate apart from his sisters, for his mien was lofty. At the age of seven he knew every question and answer in the book 'Mother's Gift,' with sayings from which he scourged sinners; and at the age of eight he delivered from memory the Book of Job at the Seiet; at that age also he was put among the elders in the Sabbath School.

He advanced, waxing great in religion. On the nights of the Saying and Searching of the Word he was with the cunningest men, disputing with the preacher, stressing his arguments with his fingers, and proving his learning with phrases from the sermons of the saintly Shones Talysarn.

If one asked him: 'What are you going, Ben Abel Deinol?' he always answered: 'The errander of the White Gospel fach.'

His father communed with the preacher, who said: 'Pity quite sinful if the boy is not in the pulpit.'

'Like that do I think as well too,' replied Abel. 'Eloquent he is. Grand he is spouting prayers at his bed. Weep do I.'

Neighbours neglected their fields and barnyards to hear the lad's shoutings to God. Once Ben opened his eyes and rebuked those who were outside his room.

'Shamed you are, not for certain,' he said to them. 'Come in, boys Capel. Right you hear the Gospel fach. Youngish am I but old is my courtship of King Jesus who died on the tree for scamps of parsons.'

He shut his eyes and sang of blood, wood, white shirts, and thorns; of the throng that would arise from the burial-ground, in which there were more graves than molehills in the shire. He cried against the heathenism of the Church, the wickedness of Church tithes, and against ungodly book-prayers and short sermons.

Early Ben entered College Carmarthen, where his piety – which was an adage – was above that of any student. Of him this was said: 'White Jesus bach is as plain on his lips as the snout of a big sow.'

Brightness fell upon him. He had a name for the tearfulness and splendour of his eloquence. He could conduct himself fancifully: now he was Pharaoh wincing under the plagues, now he was the Prodigal Son hungering at the pigs' trough, now he was the Widow of Nain rejoicing at the recovery of her son, now he was a parson in Nineveh squirming under the tongue of Jonah; and his hearers winced or hungered, rejoiced or squirmed. Congregations sought him to preach in their pulpits, and he chose such as offered the highest reward, pledging the richest men for his wage and the cost of his entertainment and journey. But Ben would rule over no chapel. 'I wait for the call from above,' he said.

His term at Carmarthen at an end, he came to Deinol. His father met him dolefully.

'An old boy very cruel is the Parson,' Abel whined. 'Has he not strained Gwen for his tithes? Auction her he did and bought her himself for three pounds and half a pound.'

Ben answered: 'Go now and say the next Saturday Benshamin Lloyd will give mouthings on tithes in Capel Dissenters.'

Ben stood in the pulpit, and he spoke to the people of Capel Dissenters.

'How many of you have been to his church?' he cried. 'Not one male bach or one female fach. Go there the next Sabbath, and the black muless will not say to you: "Welcome you are, persons Capel. But there's glad am I to see you." A comic sermon you will hear. A sermon got with half-a-crown postal order. Ask Postman. Laugh highly you will and stamp on the floor. Funny is the Parson in the white frock. Ach y fy, why for he doesn't have a coat preacher like Respecteds? Ask me that. From where does his Church come from? She is the inheritance of Satan. The only thing he had to leave, and he left her to his friends the parsons. Iss-iss, earnest affair is this. Who gives him his food? We. Who pays for his Vicarage? We. Who feeds his pony? We. His cows? We. Who built his church? We. With stones carted from our quarries and mortar messed about with the tears of our mothers and the blood of our fathers.'

At the gate of the chapel men discussed Ben's words; and two or three of them stole away and herded Gwen into the corner of the field; and they caught her and cut off her tail, and drove a staple into her udder. Sunday morning eleven men from Capel Dissenters, with iron bands to their clogs on their feet, and white aprons before their bellies, shouted without the church: 'We are come to pray from the book.' The parson was affrighted, and left over tolling his bell, and he bolted and locked the door, against which he set his body as one would set the stub of a tree.

Running at the top of their speed the railers came to Ben, telling how the Parson had put them to shame.

'Iobs you are,' Ben answered. 'The boy bach who loses the key of his house breaks into his house. Does an old wench bar the dairy to her mishtress?'

The men returned each to his abode, and an hour after midday they gathered in the church burial-ground, and they drew up a tombstone, and with it rammed the door; and they hurled stones at the windows; and in the darkness they built a wall of dung in the room of the door.

Repentance sank into the parson as he saw and remembered that which had been done to him. He called to him his servant Lissi Workhouse, and her he told to take Gwen to Deinol. The cow lowed woefully as she was driven; she was heard even in Morfa, and many hurried to the road to witness her.

Abel was at the going in of the close.

'Well-well, Lissi Workhouse,' he said, 'what's doing then?'

'"Go give the male his beast," mishtir talked.'

'Right for you are,' said Abel.

'Right for enough is the rascal. But a creature without blemish he pilfered. Hit her and hie her off.'

As Lissi was about to go, Ben cried from within the house: 'The cow the fulbert had was worth two of his cows.'

'Sure, iss-iss,' said Abel. 'Go will I to the Vicarage with boys capel. Bring the baston, Ben bach.'

Ben came out, and his ardour warmed up on beholding Lissi's broad hips, scarlet cheeks, white teeth, and full bosoms.

'Not blaming you, girl fach, am I,' he said. 'My father, journey with Gwen. Walk will I with Lissi Workhouse.'

That afternoon Abel brought a cow in calf into his close; and that night Ben crossed the mown hayfields to the Vicarage, and he threw a little gravel at Lissi's window.

★   ★   ★   ★

The hay was gathered and stacked and thatched, and the corn was cut down, and to the women who were gleaning his father's oats, Ben said how that Lissi was in the family way.

'Silence your tone, indeed,' cried one, laughing. 'No sign have I seen.'

'If I die,' observed a large woman, 'boy bach pretty innocent you are, Benshamin. Four months have I yet. And not showing much do I.'

'No,' said another, 'the bulk might be only the coil of your apron, ho-ho.'

'Whisper to us,' asked the large woman, 'who the foxer is. Keep the news will we.'

'Who but the scamp of the Parson?' replied Ben. 'What a sow of a hen.'

By such means Ben shifted his offence. On being charged by the Parson he rushed through the roads crying that the enemy of the Big Man had put unbecoming words on a harlot's tongue. Capel Dissenters believed him. 'He could not act wrongly with a sheep,' some said.

So Ben tasted the sapidness and relish of power, and his desires increased.

'Mortgage Deinol, my father bach,' he said to Abel. 'Going am I to London. Heavy shall I be there. None of the dirty English are like me.'

'Already have I borrowed for your college. No more do I want to have. How if I sell a horse?'

'Sell you the horse too, my father bach.'

'Done much have I for you,' Abel said. 'Fairish I must be with your sisters.'

'Why for you cavil like that, father? The money of mam came to Deinol. Am I not her son?'

Though his daughters murmured – 'We wake at the caw of the crows,' they said, 'and weary in the young of the day' – Abel obeyed his son, who thereupon departed and came to Thornton East to the house of Catherine Jenkins, a widow woman, with whom he took the appearance of a burning lover.

Though he preached with a view at many English chapels in London, none called him. He caused Abel to sell cattle and mortgage Deinol for what it was worth and to give him all the money he received therefrom; he swore such hot love for Catherine that the woman pawned her furniture for his sake.

Intrigued that such scant fruit had come up from his sowings, Ben thought of further ways of stablishing himself. He inquired into the welfare of shop-assistants from women and girls who worshipped in Welsh chapels, and though he spoiled several in his quest, the abominations which oppressed these workers were made known to him. Shop-assistants carried abroad his fame and called him 'Fiery Taffy.' Ben showed them how to rid themselves of their burden; 'a burden,' he said, 'packed full and overflowing by men of my race – the London Welsh drapers.'

The Welsh drapers were alarmed and in a rage with Ben. They took the opinion of their big men and performed slyly. Enos-Harries – this is the Enos-Harries who has a drapery shop in Kingsend – sent to Ben this letter: 'Take Dinner with Slf and Wife same, is Late Dinner I am pleased to inform. You we don't live in Establishment only as per printed Note Heading. And Oblige.'

Enos-Harries showed Ben his house, and told him the cost of the treasures that were therein.

Also Harries said: 'I have learned of you as a promising Welshman, and I want to do a good turn for you with a speech by you on St David's Day at Queen's Hall. Now, then.'

'I am not important enough for that.'

'She'll be a first-class miting in tip-top speeches. All the drapers and dairies shall be there in crowds. Three sirs shall come.'

'I am choked with engagements,' said Ben. 'I am preaching very busy now just.'

'Well-well. Asked I did for you are a clean Cymro bach. As I repeat, only leading lines in speakers shall be there. Come now into the drawing-room and I'll give you an intro to the Missus Enos-Harries. In evening dress she is – chik Paris Model. The invoice price was ten-ten.'

'Wait a bit,' Ben remarked. 'I would be glad if I could speak.'

'Perhaps the next time we give you the invite. The Cymrodorion shall be in the miting.'

'As you plead, try I will.'

'Stretching a point am I,' Harries said. 'This is a favour for you to address this glorious miting where the Welsh drapers will attend and the Missus Enos-Harries will sing "Land of my Fathers".'

Ben withdrew from his fellows for three days, and on the third day – which was that of the Saint – he put on him a frock coat, and combed down his moustache over the blood-red swelling on his lip; and he cleaned his teeth. Here are some of the sayings that he spoke that night:

'Half an hour ago we were privileged to listen to the voice of a lovely lady – a voice as clear as a diamond ring. It inspired us one and all with a hireath for the dear old homeland – for dear Wales, for the land of our fathers and mothers too, for the land that is our heritage not by Act of Parliament but by the Act of God...

'Who ownss this land today? The squire and the parshon. By what right? By the same right as the thief who steals your silk and your laces, and your milk and butter, and your reddymade blousis. I know a farm of one hundred acres, each rod having been tamed from heatherland into a manna of abundance. Tamed by human bones and muscles – God's invested capital in His chosen children. Six months ago this land – this fertile and rich land – was wrestled away from the owners. The bones of the living and the dead were wrestled away.

I saw it three months ago – a wylderness. The clod had been squeesed of its zweat. The land belonged to my father, and his father, and his father, back to countless generations...

'I am proud to be among my people tonight. How sorry I am for any one who are not Welsh. We have a language as ancient as the hills that shelter us, and the rivers that never weery of refreshing us...

'Only recently a few shop-assistants – a handful of counter-jumpers – tried to shake the integrity of our commerse. But their white cuffs held back their aarms, and the white collars choked their aambitions. When I was a small boy my mam used to tell me how the chief Satan was caught trying to put his hand over the sun so as to give other satans a chance of doing wrong on earth in the dark. That was the object of these misguided fools. They had no grievances. I have since investigated the questions of living-in and fines. Both are fair and necessary. The man who tries to destroy them is like the swimmer who plunges among the water lilies to be dragged into destruction...

'Welsh was talked in the Garden of Aden. That is where commerse began. Didn't Eve buy the apple?...

'Ladies and gentlemen, Cymrodorion, listen. There is a going in these classical old rafterss. It is the coming of God. And the message He gives you this night is this: "Men of Gwalia, march on and keep you tails up."'

From that hour Ben flourished. He broke his league with the shop-assistants. Those whom he had troubled lost courage and humbled themselves before their employers; but their employers would have none of them, man or woman, boy or girl.

Vexation followed his prosperity. His father reproached him, writing: 'Sad I drop into the Pool as old Abel Tybach, and not as Lloyd Deinol.' Catherine harassed him to recover her house and chattels. To these complainings he was deaf. He married the daughter of a wealthy Englishman, who set him up in a large house in the midst of a pleasure garden; and of the fatness and redness of his wife he was sickened before he was wedded to her.

By studying diligently, the English language became nearly as familiar to him as the Welsh language. He bound himself to Welsh politicians and engaged himself in public affairs, and soon he was as an idol to a multitude of people, who were sensible only to his well-sung words, and who did not know that his utterances veiled his own avarice and that of his masters. All that he did was for profit, and yet he could not win enough.

Men and women, soothed into false ease and quickened into counterfeit wrath, commended him, crying: 'Thank God for Ben Lloyd.' Such praise puffed him up, and howsoever mighty he was in the view of fools, he was mightier in his own view.

'At the next election I'll be in Parliament,' he boasted in his vanity. 'The basis of my solidity – strength – is as immovable – is as impregnable as Birds' Rock in Morfa.'

Though the grandson of Simon Idiot and Dull Anna prophesied great things for himself, it was evil that came to him.

He trembled from head to foot to ravish every comely woman on whom his ogling eyes dwelt. His greed made him faithless to those whom he professed to serve: in his eagerness to lift himself he planned, plotted, and trafficked with the foes of his officers. Hearing that an account of his misdeeds was spoken abroad, he called the high London Welshmen into a room, and he said to them:

'These cruel slanderers have all but broken my spirit. They are the wicked inventions of fiends incarnate. It is not my fall that is required – if that were so I would gladly make the sacrifise – the zupreme sacrifise, if wanted – but it is the fall of the Party that these men are after. He who repeats one foul thing is doing his level best to destroy the fabric of this magnificent organization that has been reared by your brains. It has no walls of stone and mortar, yet it is a sity builded by men. We must have no more bickerings. We have work to do. The seeds are springing forth, and a goodly harvest is promised: let us sharpen our blades and clear our barn floors. Cymru fydd – Wales for the Welsh – is here. At home and at

Westminster our kith and kin are occupying prominent positions. Disestablishment is at hand. We have closed public-houses and erected chapels, each chapel being a factor in the education of the masses in ideas of righteous government. You, my friends, have secured much of the land, around which you have made walls, and in which you have set water fountains, and have planted rare plants and flowers. And you have put up your warning signs on it – "Trespassers will be prosecuted."

'There is coming the Registration of Workers Act, by which every worker will be held to his locality, to his own enormous advantage. And it will end strikes, and trades unionism will die a dishonoured death. In future these men will be able to settle down, and with God's blessing bring children into the world, and their condition will be a delight unto themselves and a profit to the community.

'But we must do more. I must do more. And you must help me. We must stand together. Slander never creates; it shackles and kills. We must be solid. Midway off the Cardigan coast – in beautiful Morfa – there is a rock – Birds' Rock. As a boy I used to climb to the top of it, and watch the waters swirling and tumbling about it, and around it and against it. But I was unafraid. For I knew that the rock was old when man was young, and that it had braved all the washings of the sea.'

The men congratulated Ben; and Ben came home and he stood at a mirror, and shaping his body put out his arms.

'How's this for my maiden speech in the House?' he asked his wife. Presently he paused. 'You're a fine one to be an MP's lady,' he said. 'You stout, underworked fool.'

Ben urged on his imaginings: he advised his monarch, and to him for favours merchants brought their gold, and mothers their daughters. Winter and spring moved, and then his mind brought his enemies to his door.

'As the root of a tree spreads in the bosom of the earth,' he said, 'so my fame shall spread over the world'; and he built a fence about his house.

But his mind would not be stilled. Every midnight his enemies were at the fence, and he could not sleep for the dreadful outcry; every midnight he arose from his bed and walked aside the fence, testing the strength of it with a hand and a shoulder and shooing away his enemies as one does a brood of chickens from a cornfield.

His fortieth summer ran out – a season of short days and nights speeding on the heels of night. Then peace fell upon him; and at dusk of a day he came into his room, and he saw one sitting in a chair. He went up to the chair and knelt on a knee, and said: 'Your Majesty...'

## *For Better*

At the time it was said of him 'There's a boy that gets on he is,' Enoch Harries was given Gwen the daughter of the builder Dan Thomas. On the first Sunday after her marriage the people of Kingsend Welsh Tabernacle crowded about Gwen, asking her: 'How like you the bed, Messes Harries fach?' 'Enoch has opened a shop butcher then?' 'Any signs of a baban bach yet?' 'Managed to get up quickly you did the day?' Gwen answered in the manner the questions were asked, seriously or jestingly. She considered these sayings, and the cause of her uneasiness was not a puzzle to her; and she got to despise the man whom she had married, and whose skin was like parched leather, and to repel his impotent embraces.

Withal she gave Enoch pleasure. She clothed herself with costly garments, adorned her person with rings and ornaments, and she modelled her hair in the way of a bob-wig. Enoch gave in to her in all things; he took her among Welsh master builders, drapers, grocers, dairymen, into their homes and such places as they assembled in; and his pride in his wife was nearly as great as his pride in the twenty plate-glass windows of his shop.

In her vanity Gwen exalted her estate.

'I hate living over the shop,' she said. 'It's so common. Let's take a house away from here.'

'Good that I am on the premizes,' Enoch replied in Welsh. 'Hap go wrong will affairs if I leave.'

'We can't ask any one decent here. Only commercials,' Gwen said. With a show of care for her husband's welfare, she added: 'Working too hard is my boy bach. And very splendid you should be.'

Her design was fulfilled, and she and Enoch came to dwell in Thornton East, in a house near Richmond Park, and on the gate before the house, and on the door of the house, she put the name Windsor. From that hour she valued herself high. She had the words Mrs G. Enos-Harries printed on cards, and she did not speak of Enoch's trade in the hearing of anybody. She gave over conversing in Welsh, and would give no answer when spoken to in that tongue. She devised means continually to lift herself in the esteem of her neighbours, acting as she thought they acted: she had a man-servant and four maid-servants, and she instructed them to address her as the madam and Enoch as the master; she had a gong struck before meals and a bell rung during meals; the furniture in her rooms was as numerous as that in the windows of a shop; she went to the parish church on Sundays; she made feasts. But her life was bitter: tradespeople ate at her table and her neighbours disregarded her.

Enoch mollified her moaning with: 'Never mind. I could buy the whole street up. I'll have you a motor-car. Fine it will be with an advert on the front engine.'

Still slighted, Gwen smoothed her misery with deeds. She declared she was a Liberal, and she frequented Thornton Vale English Congregational Chapel. She gave ten guineas to the rebuilding fund, put a carpet on the floor of the pastor's parlour, sang at brotherhood gatherings, and entertained the pastor and his wife.

Wherefore her charity was discoursed thus: 'Now when Peter spoke of a light that shines – shines, mark you – he was thinking of such ladies as Mrs G. Enos-Harries. Not forgetting Mr G. Enos-Harries.'

'I'm going to build you a vestry,' Gwen said to the pastor. 'I'll organize a sale of work to begin with.'

The vestry was set up, and Gwen bethought of one who

should be charged with the opening ceremony of it, and to her mind came Ben Lloyd, whose repute was great among the London Welsh, and to whose house in Twickenham she rode in her car. Ben's wife answered her sharply: 'He's awfully busy. And I know he won't see visitors.'

'But won't you tell him? It will do him such a lot of good. You know what a stronghold of Toryism this place is.'

A voice from an inner room cried: 'Who is to see me?'

'Come this way,' said Mrs Lloyd.

Ben, sitting at a table with writing paper and a Bible before him, rose.

'Messes Enos-Harries,' he said, 'long since I met you. No odds if I mouth Welsh? There's a language, dear me. This will not interest you in the least. Put your ambarelo in the cornel, Messes Enos-Harries, and your backhead in a chair. Making a lecture am I.'

Gwen told him the errand upon which she was bent, and while they two drank tea, Ben said: 'Sing you a song, Messes Enos-Harries. Not forgotten have I your singing in Queen's Hall on the Day of David the Saint. Inspire me wonderfully you did with the speech. I've been sad too, but you are a wedded female. Sing you now then. Push your cup and saucer under the chair.'

'No-no, not in tone am I,' Gwen feigned.

'How about a Welsh hymn? Come in will I at the repeats.'

'Messes Lloyd will sing the piano?'

'Go must she about her duties. She's a handless poor dab.'

Gwen played and sang.

'Solemn pretty hymns have we,' said Ben. 'Are we not large?' He moved and stood under a picture which hung on the wall – his knees touching and his feet apart – and the picture was that of Cromwell. 'My friends say I am Cromwell and Milton rolled into one. The Great Father gave me a child and He took him back to the Palace. Religious am I. Want I do to live my life in the hills and valleys of Wales: listening to the anthem of creation, and searching for Him under the bark of the tree. And there I shall wait for the sound of the last trumpet.'

'A poet you are.' Gwen was astonished.

'You are a poetess, for sure me,' Ben said. He leaned over her. 'Sparkling are your eyes. Deep brown are they – brown as the nut in the paws of the squirrel. Be you a bard and write about boys Cymru. Tell how they succeed in big London.'

'I will try,' said Gwen.

'Like you are and me. Think you do as I think.'

'Know you for long I would,' said Gwen.

'For ever,' cried Ben. 'But wedded you are. Read you a bit of the lecture will I.' Having ended his reading and having sobbed over and praised that which he had read, Ben uttered: 'Certain you come again. Come you and eat supper when the wife is not at home.'

Gwen quaked as she went to her car, and she sought a person who professed to tell fortunes, and whom she made to say: 'A gentleman is in love with you. And he loves you for your brain. He is not your husband. He is more to you than your husband. I hear his silver voice holding spellbound hundreds of people; I see his majestic forehead and his auburn locks and the strands of his silken moustache.'

Those words made Gwen very happy, and she deceived herself that they were true. She composed verses and gave them to Ben.

'Not right to Nature is this,' said Ben. 'The mother is wrong. How many children you have, Messes Enos-Harries?'

'Not one. The husband is weak and he is older much than I.'

'The Father has kept His most beautiful gift from you. Pity that is.' Tears gushed from Ben's eyes. 'If the marriage-maker had brought us together, children we would have jewelled with your eyes and crowned with your hair.'

'And your intellect,' said Gwen. 'You will be the greatest Welshman.'

'Whisper will I now. A drag is the wife. Happy you are with the husband.'

'Why for you speak like that?'

'And for why we are not married?' Ben took Gwen in his arms and he kissed her and drew her body nigh to him; and in a little while he opened the door sharply and rebuked his wife that she waited thereat.

Daily did Gwen praise and laud Ben to her husband. 'There is no one in the world like him,' she said. 'He will get very far.'

'Bring Mistar Lloyd to Windsor for me to know him quite well,' said Enoch.

'I will ask him,' Gwen replied without faltering.

'Benefit myself I will.'

Early every Thursday afternoon Ben arrived at Windsor, and at the coming home from his shop of Enoch, Ben always said: 'Messes Enos-Harries has been singing the piano. Like the trilling of God's feathered choir is her music.'

Though Ben and Gwen were left at peace they could not satisfy nor crush their lust.

Before three years were over, Ben had obtained great fame. 'He ought to be in Parliament and give up preaching entirely,' some said; and Enoch and Gwen were partakers of his glory.

Then Gwen told him that she had conceived, whereof Ben counselled her to go into her husband's bed.

'That I have not the stomach to do,' the woman complained.

'As you say, dear heart,' said Ben. 'Cancer has the wife. Perish soon she must. Smooth our path and lie with your lout.'

Presently Gwen bore a child; and Enoch her husband looked at it and said: "Going up is Ben Lloyd. Solid am I as the counter.'

Gwen related her fears to Ben, who contrived to make Enoch a member of the London County Council. Enoch rejoiced: summoning the congregation of Thornton Vale to be witnesses of his gift of a Bible cushion to the chapel.

As joy came to him, so grief fell upon his wife. 'After all,' Ben wrote to her, 'you belong to him. You have been joined together in the holiest and sacredest matrimony. Monumental responsibilities have been thrust on me by my people. I did not seek for them, but it is my duty to bear them. Pray that I shall use God's hoe with understanding and wisdom. There is talk of putting me up for Parliament. Voters will have a chance of electing a real religious man. I must not be tempted by you again. Well, good-bye, Gwen, may He keep you unspotted from the world. Ships that pass in the night.'

Enoch was plagued, and he followed Ben to chapel meetings, eisteddfodau, Cymrodorion and St David's Day gatherings, always speaking in this fashion: 'Cast under is the girl fach you do not visit her. Improved has her singing.'

Because Ben was careless of his call, his wrath heated and he said to him: 'Growing is the baban.'

'How's trade?' Ben remarked. 'Do you estimate for Government contracts?'

'Not thought have I.'

'Just hinted. A word I can put in.'

'Red is the head of the baban.'

'Two black heads make red,' observed Ben.

'And his name is Benjamin.'

'As you speak. Farewell for today. How would you like to put up for a Welsh constituency?'

'Not deserving am I of anything. Happy would I and the wife be to see you in the House.'

But Ben's promise was fruitless; and Enoch bewailed: 'A serpent flew into my house.'

He ordered Gwen to go to Ben.

'Recall to him this and that,' he said. 'Say that a splendid advert an MP would be for the business. Be you dressed like a lady. Take a fur coat on appro from the shop.'

Often thereafter he bade his wife to take such a message. But Gwen had overcome her distress and she strew abroad her charms; for no man could now suffice her. So she always departed to one of her lovers and came back with fables on her tongue.

'What can you expect of the Welsh?' cried Enoch in his wrath. 'He hasn't paid for the goods he got on tick from the shop. County court him will I. He ate my food. The unrighteous ate the foot of the righteous. And he was bad with you. Did I not watch? No good is the assistant that lets the customer go away with not a much obliged.'

The portion of the Bible that Enoch read that night was this:

'I have decked my bed with coverings of tapestry, with carved works, with fine linen of Egypt... Come, let us take our fill of love until the morning: let us solace ourselves with love. For the goodman is not at home, he is gone on a long journey. He hath –'

'That's lovely,' said Gwen.

'Tapestry from my shop,' Enoch expounded. 'And Irish linen. And busy was the draper in Kingsend.'

Gwen pretended to be asleep.

'He is the father. That will learn him to keep his promise, the wicked man.'

Unknown to her husband Gwen stood before Ben; and at the sight of her Ben longed to wanton with her. Gwen stretched out her arms to be clear of him and to speak to him; her speech was stopped with kisses and her breasts swelled out. Again she found pleasure in Ben's strength.

Then she spoke of her husband's hatred.

'Like a Welshman every spit he is,' said Ben. 'And a black.'

But his naughtiness oppressed him for many days and he intrigued; and it came to pass that Enoch was asked to contest a Welsh constituency, and Enoch immediately let fall his anger for Ben.

'Celebrate this we shall with a reception in the Town Hall,' he announced. 'You, Gwen fach, will wear the chikest Paris model we can find. Ben's kindness is more than I expected. Much that I have I owe to him.'

'Even your son,' said Gwen.

# Saint David and the Prophets

God grants prayers gladly. In the moment that Death was aiming at him a missile of down, Hughes-Jones prayed: 'Bad I've been. Don't let me fall into the Fiery Pool. Give me a brief while and a grand one I'll be for the religion.' A shaft of fire came out of the mouth of the Lord and the shaft stood in the way of the missile, consuming it utterly; 'So,' said the Lord, 'are his offences forgotten.'

'Is it a light thing,' asked Paul, 'to defy the Law?'

'God is merciful,' said Moses.

'Is the Kingdom for such as pray conveniently?'

'This,' Moses reproved Paul, 'is written in a book: "The Lord shall judge His people."'

Yet Paul continued to dispute, the Prophets gathering near him for entertainment; and the company did not break up until God, as is the custom in Heaven when salvation is wrought, proclaimed a period of rejoicing.

Wherefore Heaven's windows, the number of which is more than that of blades of grass in the biggest hayfield, were lit as with a flame; and Heman and his youths touched their instruments with fingers and hammers and the singing angels lifted their voices in song; and angels in the likeness of young girls brewed tea in urns and angels in the likeness of old women baked pleasant breads in the heavenly ovens. Out of Hell there arose two mountains, which established themselves one over the other on the floor of Heaven, and the height of the mountains was the depth of Hell; and you could not see the sides of the mountains for the vast multitude of sinners thereon, and you could not see the sinners for the live coals to which they were held, and you could not see the burning coals for the radiance of the pulpit which was set on the furthermost peak of the mountain, and you could not see the pulpit – from toe to head it was of pure gold – for the shining countenance of Isaiah; and as Isaiah preached, blood issued out of the ends of his fingers from the violence with which he smote his Bible, and his single voice was louder than the lamentations of the damned.

As the Lord had enjoined, the inhabitants of Heaven rejoiced: eating and drinking, weeping and crying hosanna.

But Paul would not joy over that which the Lord had done, and soon he sought Him, and finding Him said: 'A certain Roman noble laboured his horses to their death in a chariot race before Cæsar: was he worthy of Cæsar's reward?'

'The noble is on the mountain-side,' God answered, 'and his horses are in my chariots.'

'One bears witness to his own iniquity, and you bid us feast and you say "He shall have remembrance of me."'

'Is there room in Heaven for a false witness?' asked God.

Again did Paul seek God. 'My Lord,' he entreated, 'what manner of man is this that confesses his faults?'

'You will provoke my wrath,' said God. 'Go and be merry.'

Paul's face being well turned, God moved backward into the Record Office, and of the Clerk of the Records He demanded: 'Who is he that prayed unto me?'

'William Hughes-Jones,' replied the Clerk.

'Has the Forgiving Angel blotted out his sins?'

'For that I have fixed a long space of time'; and the Clerk showed God eleven heavy books, on the outside of each of which was written: 'William Hughes-Jones, One and All Drapery Store, Hammersmith. His sins'; and God examined the books and was pleased, and He cried: 'Rejoice fourfold'; and if Isaiah's roar was higher than the wailings of the perished it was now more awful than the roar of a hundred bullocks in a slaughter-house, and if Isaiah's countenance shone more than anything in Heaven, it was now like the eye of the sun.

'Of what nation is he?' the Lord inquired of the Clerk.

'The Welsh; the Welsh Nonconformists.'

'Put before me their good deeds.'

'There is none. William Hughes-Jones is the first of them that has prayed. Are not the builders making a chamber for the accounts of their disobedience?'

Immediately God thundered: the earth trembled and the stars shivered and fled from their courses and struck against one another; and God stood on the brim of the universe and stretched out a hand and a portion of a star fell into it, and that is the portion which He hurled into the garden of Hughes-Jones's house. On a sudden the revels ceased: the bread of the feast was stone and the tea water, and the songs of the angels were hushed, and the strings of the harps and viols were withered, and the hammers were dough, and the mountains sank into Hell, and behold Satan in the pulpit which was an iron cage.

The Prophets hurried into the Judgment Hall with questions, and lo God was in a cloud, and He spoke out of the cloud.

'I am angry,' He said, 'that Welsh Nonconformists have not heard my name. Who are the Welsh Nonconformists?' The Prophets were silent, and God mourned: 'My Word is the earth and I peopled the earth with my spittle; and I appointed my Prophets to watch over my people, and the watchers slept and my children strayed.'

Thus too said the Lord: 'That hour I devour my children who have forsaken me, that hour I shall devour my Prophets.'

'May be there is one righteous among us?' said Moses.

'You have all erred.'

'May be there is one righteous among the Nonconformists,' said Moses; 'will the just God destroy him?'

'The one righteous is humbled, and I have warned him to keep my commandments.'

'The sown seed brought forth a prayer,' Moses pleaded; 'will not the just God wait for the harvest?'

'My Lord is just,' Paul announced. 'They who gather wickedness shall not escape the judgment, nor shall the blind instructor be held blameless.'

Moreover Paul said: 'The Welsh Nonconformists have been informed of you as is proved by the man who confessed his transgressions. It is a good thing for me that I am not of the Prophets.'

'I'll be your comfort, Paul,' the Prophets murmured, 'that you have done this to our hurt.' Abasing themselves, they tore their mantles and howled; and God, piteous of their howlings, was constrained to say: 'Bring me the prayers of these people and I will forget your remissness.'

The Prophets ran hither and thither, wailing; 'Woe. Woe. Woe.'

Sore that they behaved with such scant respect, Paul herded them into the Council Room. 'Is it seemly,' he rebuked them, 'that the Prophets of God act like madmen?'

'Our lot is awful,' said they.

'The lot of the backslider is justifiably awful,' was Paul's reminder. 'You have prophesied too diligently of your own glory.'

'You are learned in the Law, Paul,' said Moses. 'Make us waywise.'

'Send abroad a messenger to preach damnation to sinners,' answered Paul. 'For Heaven,' added he, 'is the knowledge of Hell.'

So it came to pass. From the hem of Heaven's Highway an angel flew into Wales; and the angel, having judged by his sight and his hearing, returned to the Council Room and testified to the godliness of the Welsh Nonconformists. 'As difficult for me,' he vowed, 'to write the feathers of my wings as the sum of their daily prayers.'

'None has reached the Record Office,' said Paul.

'They are always engaged in this bright business,' the angel declared, 'and praising the Lord. And the number of the people is many and Heaven will need be enlarged for their coming.'

'Of a surety they pray?' asked Paul.

## Saint David and the Prophets

'Of a surety. And as they pray they quake terribly.'

'The Romans prayed hardly,' said Paul. 'But they prayed to other gods.'

'Wherever you stand on their land,' asserted the angel, 'you see a temple.'

'I exceedingly fear,' Paul remarked, 'that another Lord has dominion over them.'

The Prophets were alarmed, and they sent a company of angels over the earth and a company under the earth; and the angels came back; one company said: 'We searched the swampy marges and saw neither a god nor a heaven nor any prayer,' and the other company said: 'We probed the lofty emptiness and we did not touch a god or a heaven or any prayer.'

Paul was distressed and he reported his misgivings to God, and God upbraided the Prophets for their sloth. 'Is there no one who can do this for me?' He cried. 'Are all the cunning men in Hell? Shall I make all Heaven drink the dregs of my fury? Burnish your rusted armour. Depart into Hell and cry out: "Is there one here who knows the Welsh Nonconformists?" Choose the most crafty and release him and lead him here.'

Lots were cast and it fell to Moses to descend into Hell; and he stood at the well, the water of which is harder than crystal, and he cried out; and of the many that professed he chose Saint David, whom he brought up to God.

'Visit your people,' said God to the Saint, 'and bring me their prayers.'

'Why should I be called?'

'It is my will. My Prophets have failed me, and if it is not done they shall be destroyed.'

David laughed. 'From Hell comes a saviour of the Prophets. In the middle of my discourse at the Judgment Seat the Prophets stooped upon me. "To Hell with him," they screamed.'

'Perform faithfully,' said the Lord, 'and you shall remain in Paradise.'

'My Lord is gracious! I was a Prophet and the living believe that I am with the saints. I will retire.'

'Perform faithfully and you shall be of my Prophets.'

Then God took away David's body and nailed it upon a wall, and He put wings on the shoulders of his soul; and David darted through a cloud and landed on earth, and having looked at the filthiness of the Nonconformists in Wales he withdrew to London. But however actively he tried he could not find a man of God nor the destination of the fearful prayers of Welsh preachers, grocers, drapers, milkmen, lawyers, and politicians.

Loth to go to Hell and put to a nonplus, David built a nest in a tree in Richmond Park, and he paused therein to consider which way to proceed. One day he was disturbed by the singing and preaching of a Welsh soldier who had taken shelter from rain under the tree. David came down from his nest, and when the mouth of the man was most open, he plunged into the fellow's body. Henceforward in whatsoever place the soldier was there also was David; and the soldier carried him to a clothier's shop in Putney, the sign of the shop being written in this fashion:

J, PARKER LEWIS.
The Little (Gents. Mercer) Wonder.

Crossing the threshold, the soldier shouted: 'How you are?'

The clothier, whose skin was as hide which has been scorched in a tanner's yard, bent over the counter. 'Man bach,' he exclaimed, 'glad am I to see you. Pray will I now that you are all Zer Garnett.' His thanksgiving finished, he said: 'Wanting a suit you do.'

'Yes, and no,' replied the soldier. 'Cheap she must be if yes.'

'You need one for certain. Shabby you are.'

'This is a friendly call. To a low-class shop must a poor tommy go.'

'Do you then not be cheated by an English swindler.' The clothier raised his thin voice: 'Kate, here's a strange boy.'

A pretty young woman, in spite of her snaggled teeth, frisked into the room like a wanton lamb. Her brown hair was drawn carelessly over her head, and her flesh was packed but loosely.

'Serious me,' she cried, 'Llew Eevans! Llew bach, how you are? Very big has the army made you and strong.'

'Not changed you are.'

'No. The last time you came was to see the rabbit.'

'Dear me, yes. Have you still got her?'

'She's in the belly long ago,' said the clothier.

'I have another in her stead,' said Kate. 'A splendid one. Would you like to fondle her?'

'Why, yez,' answered the soldier.

'Drat the old animal,' cried the clothier. 'Too much care you give her, Kate. Seven looks has the deacon from Capel King's Cross had of her and he hasn't bought her yet.'

As he spoke the clothier heaped garments on the counter.

'Put out your arms,' he ordered Kate, 'and take the suits to a room for Llew to try on.'

Kate obeyed, and Llew hymning 'Moriah' took her round the waist and embraced her, and the woman, hungering for love, gladly gave herself up. Soon attired in a black frock coat, a black waistcoat, and black trousers, Llew stepped into the shop.

'A champion is the rabbit,' he said; 'and very tame.'

'If meat doesn't come down,' said the clothier, 'in the belly she'll be as well.'

'Let me know before you slay her. Perhaps I buy her. I will study her again.'

The clothier gazed upon Llew. 'Tidy fit,' he said.

'A bargain you give me.'

'Why for you talk like that?' the clothier protested. 'No profit can I make on a Cymro. As per invoice is the cost. And a latest style bowler hat I throw in.'

Peering through Llew's body, Saint David saw that the dealer dealt treacherously, and that the money which he got for the garments was two pounds over that which was proper.

Llew walked away whistling. 'A simple fellow is the black,' he said to himself. 'Three soverens was bad.'

On the evening of the next day – that day being the Sabbath

– the soldier worshipped in Capel Kingsend; and betwixt the sermon and the benediction, the preacher delivered this speech: 'Very happy am I to see so many warriors here once more. We sacrificed for them quite a lot, and if they have any Christianity left in them they will not forget what Capel Kingsend has done and will repay same with interest. Happier still we are to welcome Mister Hughes-Jones to the Big Seat. In the valley of the shadow has Mister Hughes-Jones been. Earnestly we prayed for our dear religious leader. Tomorrow at seven we shall hold a prayer meeting for his cure. At seven at night. Will everybody remember? On Monday – tomorrow – at seven at night a prayer meeting for Mister Hughes-Jones will be held in Capel Kingsend. The duty of every one is to attend. Will you please say something now, zer?'

Hughes-Jones rose from the arm-chair which is under the pulpit, and thrust out his bristled chin and rested his palms on the communion table; and he said not one word.

'Mister Hughes-Jones,' the preacher urged.

'I am too full of grace,' said Hughes-Jones; he spoke quickly, as one who is on the verge of tears, and his big nostrils widened and narrowed as those of one who is short of breath.

'The congregation, zer, expects –'

'Well-well, I've had a glimpse of the better land and with a clear conscience I could go there, only the Great Father has more for me to do here. A miracle happened to me. In the thick of my sickness a meetority dropped outside the bedroom. The mistress fainted slap bang. "If this is my summons," I said, "I am ready." A narrow squeak that was. I will now sit and pray for you one and all.'

In the morning Llew went to the One and All and in English – that is the tongue of the high Welsh – did he address Hughes-Jones.

'I've come to start, zer,' he said.

'Why wassn't you in the chapel yezterday?'

'I wass there, zer.'

'Ho-ho. For me there are two people in the chapel – me and Him.'

'Yez, indeed. Shall I gommence now?'
'Gommence what?'
'My crib what I leave to join up.'
'Things have changed. There has been a war on, mister. They are all smart young ladies here now. And it is not right to sack them and shove them on the streets.'
'But –'
'Don't answer back, or I'll have you chucked from the premizes and locked up. Much gratitude you show for all I did for the soders.'
'Beg pardon, zer.'
'We too did our bits at home. Slaved like horses. Me and the two sons. And they had to do work of national importance. Disgraceful I call it in a free country.'
'I would be much obliged, zer, if you would take me on.'
'You left on your own accord, didn't you? I never take back a hand that leave on their own. Why don't you be patriotic and rejoin and finish up the Huns?'

Bowed down, the soldier made himself drunk, and the drink enlivened his dismettled heart; and in the evening he stole into the loft which is above the Big Seat of Capel Kingsend, purposing to disturb the praying men with loud curses.

But Llew slept, and while he slept the words of the praying men came through the ceiling like the pieces of a child's jig-saw puzzle; some floated sluggishly and fell upon the wall and the roof, and some because of their little strength did not reach above the floor; and none went through the roof. Saint David closed his hands on many, and there was no soundness in them, and they became as though they were nothing. He formed a bag of the soldier's handkerchief, and he filled it with the words, but as he drew to the edges they crumbled into less than dust.

He pondered; and he made a sack out of cobwebs, and when the sack could not contain any more words, he wove a lid of cobwebs over the mouth of it. Jealous that no mishap should befall his treasure, he mounted a low, slow-moving cloud, and folding his wings rode up to the Gate of the Highway.

## Your Sin Will Find You Out

A Welsh youth was going to be a preacher, and his name was Joseph. In his twentieth year Adah took him to petty sessions.

'He is the data of my female child,' said Adah.

The justices were parson church and other churchers.

'Say your say, Joseph,' said parson.

'Well,' said Joseph, 'she is two times my years and two times my length and she took me into cowhouse and not know did I she was teaching me bad.'

'Half-a-crown a week,' said parson.

Joseph reported the matter to the Big Man, and the Big Man spoke to him in the language of the Garden of Eden, which was Welsh.

'Blockhead is parson,' he said. 'His religion is in his back head. Do not pay the wench.'

'All right you are,' said Joseph.

Then Adah sent a policeman after him, and he was afraid and cried out:

'Little Big Man, remember me!'

'For why you did not name another man for the father? There's a dolt for you.'

'Off you are, Big Man, in your head. Is a capel preacher to be then a dolt? For shame, for shame! Put on your think and help me.'

The Big Man repented.

'Make you I will, Jos bach, a preacher blown full.'
'I have not been to college for the B.A.'
'I will give you the soap religious. Open your mouth.'

Joseph did so and the Big Man put soap religious in his pipe-neck.

'Now you have the speech of a capel prophet,' said the Big Man, 'bubbles and suds.'

'Large thanks.'

'This I do because you are capel,' said the Big Man, 'but if you sin once more I will dry the soap and slap-bang you into Hell. Go and wash my people on the high hills where Adah cannot find you, and have whiskers on your face in a hurry. Pelt off in the night on the sly that nobody can see you to tell your road to Adah. There is no mercy in the heart of a cheapened woman. So long, Jos bach.'

Capellers knew that Joseph's going was Adah's doing, and the big heads broke the woman from capel, for it is a dirty sin to bring the law on a preacher to be. Thus the woman was proved a baddess and no one would have to do with her, and she left the neighbourhood to seek a place where her iniquity was not known.

For thirty years Joseph took the Medicine to forlorn people on hill-tops. He was called Pilgrim Whiskers. His beard was long and thick and when he neared a house he sang the hymn that begins:

> A pilgrim in a foreign land
> Both near and far I roam,
> Expecting every hour to see
> My Father's glorious home.

In the heavy heat of a Sunday evening in June he came to a remote house. He looked at it and knew the plan of it: at one end two rooms for humans and a loft reached by a ladder, at the other end a henroost and a dairy, between a cowhouse with two tie-stalls. Hens pecked and two pigs snouted in its close, and two cows were lying in a field beyond. Joseph sang his hymn in a deep belly voice, and no person appearing he put his trust in the Big Man and went into the henroost. While he was swallowing eggs he heard a voice saying:

'Who are you?'

'Pilgrim Whiskers am I,' he answered.

'You don't say!' cried the voice gladly. 'Bring you the Medicine then to me.'

Joseph passed through the cowhouse and came to a lusty woman who was sitting on a three-legged stool under a canopied chimney. Her knees clasped the pole of a scythe and she was stoning the blade of it.

'Heavy is your hand for sharpening, old woman,' said Joseph. 'I will sharpen.'

He took the blade from the pole and began to stone it, saying in the while:

'Hay you have to cut, old woman. What of your religious hay? What is your crop for the crooked man with the crooked pole to harvest?'

The woman mumbled sorrowfully:

'Brambles and thorns, dandelions and thistles are my harvest.'

Joseph cut a hair of his beard with the blade.

'What an edge!' he said. 'Fit for the crooked man!'

'Pilgrim Whiskers,' said the woman, 'true you wash poor dabs white?'

'White as the white shirt of Heaven.'

'Here's fortunate! Bet the daughter is in Capel Bethel. Stay you and she will give you eats. Sinnesses we are. Where we rest the capel finds our sin and no rest we have.'

'That is the law – the law religious. Their sin does not go before sinners. Ho-no. It goes after them. Bible say is "Your sin will find you out."'

The man and woman sat opposite each other and a smouldering pile of peat and wood was between them, and over the pile a pot of foodstuff hung; but the man did not know the woman for Adah or she him for Joseph.

'As you climb the up-ladder to the loft, so sinners climb to Heaven,' Joseph said, 'but their sin catches them on top and knocks them to Hell.'

'Little Pilgrim Whiskers, wash us,' entreated the woman.

'If curing a cow is costly,' said Joseph, 'how much more costly one pair of two black sinnesses?'

Adah brought from the lower room a calico purse.

'The whole of my money,' she said. 'Do not count lest the whole is too little, good man.'

'Tinkly is the jingle and thin the purse. No odds. Big Man, hymnful and fat is the old woman's purse for you. Shall I wash her?'

'Yes-yes. Amen and amen.'

'Wash you I will white in the blood of your sin.'

'There's happy am I.'

Joseph spat against the pot and chanted the following:

'Going to Heaven you are. What a Heaven is Heaven! No land to plough, no shirt to wet or sweat, no tatoes to blight, no cows to milk on frosty mornings, no shops with short weights, no greedy landlord, no cruel tax-gatherer, no collections on Sundays, no mouthy big heads. Capel is Heaven. A yellow capel is Heaven. The Big Man made colours and he painted Capel Heaven with the brightest yellow and the others he threw into the drab old rainbow.'

'Alelwia!' cried Adah joyously.

Bet came from Bethel and heedless of the stranger she told her woe.

'Mammo fach nice,' she said, 'do not you go into a faint at the hear of a babbler in Bethel. You have me and I have you and no matter the big heads broke us out this night.'

'Daughter fach,' said the mother, 'be not down for my news is high. Listen, frogs Bethel, Pilgrim Whiskers has washed me white. With Heaven's soap he will wash Bet.'

'Heaven has no soap to wash out a capel judgment,' said Bet.

'Gabble not. Get you ready food for Pilgrim's belly.'

Bet stepped up the ladder to the loft and returned in her workday clothes. She stirred the peat and wood, and brought bowls and spoons and bread; and she tipped the pot and filled a bucket with the mess and put it aside for the pigs in the morning.

'Take you a bowl,' she said to Pilgrim.

Pilgrim did this and filled it from the pot, and Adah did likewise and also Bet.

Having eaten, Pilgrim went to the door.

'Far sight is near rain,' he said. 'Very plain are the breasts of the far hills. Your cows make sure of dry beds before the storom.'

'Will you not have a dry bed?' said Adah.

Bet looked into Pilgrim's eyes and then inclined her own.

'Journey you must,' she said. 'Have your hat on your head.'

'The religious halo is my hat,' said Pilgrim. 'As you tell, I must journey. Thanks for now.'

He left.

Bet shooed the fowls to roost and the pigs to their sty, and she came in and lit a candle.

'Gone is the tramp,' she said.

She blew out the candle by and by and went to her bed in the loft and Adah went to hers in the lower room.

Presently Adah called:

'Bet! Betfach!'

'Yea, mammo?'

'Pelting is rain and storm is brewing. Hap man Pilgrim is Iesu Grist and you sent him away.'

'An old tramp he is with lazy broad thighs.'

After a short while Adah called again:

'A sound on the door. Hap Iesu Grist is tapping with an angel's feather. Who knows? Who knows?'

Bet descended in her nightgown, lit the candle, and opened the door; and the Pilgrim was thereat.

He crossed the threshold without her bidding; and Adah cried in her bed:

'Glad am I of you in my house and how your shirt?'

'The shirt is my skin,' Pilgrim replied.

'Dry the shirt with fire, Bet, and lie on it in bed. A morning comfort is a flesh-warmed shirt.'

Pilgrim bent and Bet drew the shirt over his head, and the candlelight lit his hairy chest. She shifted the candle and turned to the fire, and she held the shirt before it.

Pilgrim sprawled sideways on the hearth.
'What is the tune of the rain, think you?' he murmured softly.
'Hoity me! No singer am I.'
'A courting song is song rain.'
Bet did not say anything to that.
'Black as my hair is your hair and dark as my face is your face,' said Pilgrim. 'Are not my words very warm?'
'Then why for you do not dry your shirt with them?'
'A short wench fach you are, but husband-high.'
'Think you I am a wench who courts in bed? Well-well no.'
'I knocked at your door, morsel, and you opened.'
'Mammo bade me open.'
'You opened me in. Will you open me out now night is down?'
'Close your bad lips.'
'There's steam in my body. Strong is the steam. Smell you not a man?'
'No-no, I will not look or smell. I will sleep on your shirt.'
She took the shirt to the loft, and she drew the trap-door over the hole.
Pilgrim removed his shoes.
'Quiet you are, Bet!' cried Adah. 'Do not tell Iesu Grist has gone!'
'Silence your tongue, old woman,' said Pilgrim. 'In the pang of wash sin is the daughter.'
At that the soap in his neck dried; and Adah knew the voice and rose from her bed, and when she came into the room he was on the ladder.
'Where you go, you very religious Pilgrim Whiskers?' she said.
'A chatterer you are, old woman! Does the shepherd care no more for the sheep he has dipped? Yes-yes. Peril is in the night. I will guard my little sheep from peril.'
'Like would I a prayer,' said Adah.
Pilgrim came down and knelt.
'Bow your head, Pilgrim,' said Adah. 'Bow to the ground for to make a solemn prayer.'

When his head was bowed low, she went astride his back and held his shoulders with her knees, and she took the blade of the scythe and put the edge on his neck.

'The woman Adah am I,' she said.

'Big Man, remember me,' said Pilgrim. 'Tens of twelves have I washed with your soap religious.'

'Big Man,' said Adah, 'perished have I every minute of twenty-and-ten years.'

'Big Man,' said Pilgrim, 'a sin in the think is a sin undone.'

'Big Man,' said Adah, 'from a seed the thistle grows.'

'Big Man,' said Pilgrim, 'Bet has my shirt in her bed for to teach me bad.'

'Big Man,' said Adah, 'is a sinner taught the same sin twice?'

'Big Man,' said Pilgrim, 'wither at once in a hurry the old woman's heavy hands and stop the knife to keep my life.'

'Big Man,' said Adah, 'strengthen my hands with your anger.'

'Big Man,' said Pilgrim, 'remember your pilgrim in a foreign land, both near and –'

Pilgrim's head fell away.

Then Adah called her daughter, saying:

'The blood of sin washes white. Let us wash.'

# Changeable as a Woman with Child

A buxom woman with thin lips and large eyes married a sheepish redhead who wore a rope of hair round his neck. She was Katrin and he was Ianto, and whereas she married him for love, he married her for land.

'Up and down from your bed,' he commanded her on the morning after their marriage. 'Night will soon be here.'

The nights were too long and the days too short for him and he drove his wife as hard as he drove himself. They ate when they were famished and fell on their bed when they could not stand. In three years he was grown fat and his neck bearded, and she was become rags and bones; and she did not sleep with him because she was afraid she would strangle him with his beard.

On a frosty day she was making butter and baking bread, and he was in a fretful mood that he was kept from the land.

'Frozen is the poor earth down in the belly,' he remarked dismally.

She plucked a loaf from the oven, tapped and tossed it, and finding it was baked, laid it aside.

He looked through a small window and said to the land: 'Sun and rain spring will stir your little belly with life.'

'Shut your head,' said Katrin. 'How can the belly stir without you sow seed?'

He had no ear for words that did not run from his own tongue.

'Why for does not the frost go when there is ploughing to be done?' he asked himself aloud.

'Hoi-hoi and hoi-hoi,' sighed the woman. 'A one of a iob you are. Hard is the earth and foolish are we to be her slaves. She takes us in life and marries us in death.'

'A hare I see! What right has he on my land! One hare and there will be five, ten-and-twenty, one hundred! One hundred hares eating my corn and grass and turnips!'

He loaded his gun and went after the hare.

Katrin peeled potatoes for the night meal of squashed potatoes and buttermilk, and put them in a pot and hooked it over a log fire.

The day darkened and the moon rose, and she drew a shawl over her head and went with buckets to the pistil five hundred yards distant on the highway; and while she waited upon the trickling water, a swarthy man came along and said he would like to drink.

'Yes,' she said, 'drink you, strange mouth.'

'After your buckets are filled,' said the man, 'will I drink.'

'Who you are?'

'A male man.'

'Where are you going?'

'North.'

'Say where north?'

'Half north.'

'There's close you are. Evil is the secret in a close man's head.'

'A journeyman am I, and I have heard telling of jobbins in factory flannel Shinkin.'

'Ten-and-twenty miles is Aberystwyth and ten beyond is factory flannel Shinkin. The buckets are brimming. Drink you.'

The weaver raised a bucket to his heavy lips.

Katrin gaped in astonishment.

'Soft as a weaver's arms is the saying,' she said. 'But, man-man, hefty you are.'

'Go you my road?'

'For a while, ho-yes.'
'I will carry the buckets.'
They walked together, he as if he was carrying nothing.
'Lonely your travel,' said Katrin. 'Hap you slip and will you look to the moon for help?'
'Moon man will not forsake me.'
Katrin paused on a sudden.
'Give me the buckets,' she said sharply. 'Go on, wayfarer.'
'No. I will carry.'
The man hummed a hymn tune.
'Off with you to the wife that belongs to you!' said Katrin.
'Not in wedlock am I.'
'As you say.'
'Here and there is a journeyman's bed and his wife is a widow before his funeral.'
'Ho – well. This is my gate.' Katrin lifted the latch.
'Have your buckets,' said the weaver.
'Half done kindness is no kindness,' said Katrin. 'Will you not bring them to the door?'
At the door the weaver said:
'Have your buckets.'
Katrin opened the door.
'Come you in. Sit your back head on the settle for a warm.'
'Well, I will. Comfortable is a fire.'
She put a bib apron over her shawl and coiled her skirt that she should look fatter.
'And yet you run from comfort, weaver. Sup you tatoes and buttermilk and bread.'
Having eaten, the weaver said:
'I am away now.'
'Weaver! Weaver bach, graceless is the man who finishes his feast and puts on his cap. Be not in a haste. The husband is hunting the hare and we will hear his feet on the frosty ground.'
'Large thanks for the eats and far'well.'
Katrin threw logs on the fire and picked up bellows and blew them, chanting:
'Little bellows, little bellows, which way the weaver goes?

Blow north. Ho-no. Blow south. Ho-no. Blow east. Ho-no. Blow west. Ho-no. Little bellows, little bellows, which way the weaver goes? Weaver, the bellows blow to bed.'

'Comforted am I,' said the weaver. 'I am away.'

Katrin bent her body and hipped her hands, saying:

'A dull weaver you are you cannot see a pattern. Comforted! Can a man be comforted by the belly alone? Bread for strength and buttermilk for imagining and "I am away" you babble.'

'Large thanks and if a service I can do for you, call me.'

'Hap you will come this part again?' asked Katrin.

'Hap, yes.'

'Then pass you,' she said scornfully. 'No heat you will have even though your nose be a spout ice.'

The weaver was nonplussed.

'How have I crossed you?' he asked. 'Sorry am I.'

'Sorry am I for a man toop,' said Katrin loftily. 'I have two beds and give you one. But for you a road stuffed with ice than a bed with feathers.'

The weaver sat on and slumber overtook him.

'Stay I will,' he said. 'Show me now the tempting bed with soft feathers.'

'Lead you I will.'

Katrin went before him up a stairway.

'Fair night,' said the weaver.

'So long for now,' said Katrin.

She brought down Ianto's nightshirt and put it in the oven.

Presently Ianto returned. He put a hare's ear in the fire.

'There is an old hare now!' he said. 'I shoot off his ear and he is not killed. But I will catch him.'

He ate while Katrin removed his leggings and boots and corduroy trousers.

'Dear me,' she said, 'here's mud.'

'Rain is tumbling into the belly.'

'Now just a trampin begged and I gave him stale bread and sent him to the cowhouse.'

'I tramp after hare and a trampin eats my bread,' said Ianto. 'I will make the trampin plough on the morrow.'

His garments were removed, other than shirt, stockings, and drawers, and the nightshirt was dropped over his head, and he made towards the stairs.

Katrin was repentant of her mind.

'I will bed with you this night,' she said.

'Stoof and no sense!' he said. 'Call me early for to kill the hare.'

After he was gone, Katrin sat by the fire, saying 'Yes' and 'No.' In an hour she was in the weaver's room.

'Weaver bach,' she said. 'Weaver bach, wake you.'

The man awoke.

'What is in your think?' she said.

'Sin, woe me,' he answered.

'If two thinks are filled with one think, is that a sin?'

'Yes, indeed.'

'How do we know a sin is a sin before we have sinned? Tell me that.'

'There is no tell to that. The husband?'

'He sleeps in his two ears. Deafer he is than an adder and blinder than a mole.'

At the first streaks of dawn the weaver said:

'Run will I.'

'The husband may see you and take you for the hare. Go down silently and come in and I will breakfast you, and thank you the husband for bread and a straw bed.'

The weaver went out and returned, and said:

'I ate your bread and rested in your cowhouse.'

Ianto, who was eating, gazed upon him.

'Smooth are your hands,' he said. 'Blister them for your bread.'

He took him to a field of pasture and harnessed two mares to a plough.

'Break this field,' he said, 'and I go hunt the hare I lost.'

The weaver was no ploughman. He shouted at his mares and they trotted and the plough knocked him about and he could scarce get its nose into the earth.

Presently Katrin came to see how he did.

'You plough the wind,' she said. She took the plough and began to make a furrow, speaking the while. 'The plougher is gentle with his horses and firm with the plough, and his eyes are beyond for straightness.'

There was the sound of a shot, and a hare ran to the shelter of the plough.

'A hare with one ear!' cried the weaver. 'Hare, hare, are you a good or bad omen?'

'Be good to a hurt hare and good will come to you,' said Katrin. 'In peril you are, hare. Shooting for to kill you is the husband. Hie you to the moor. For sure there the grass is tough and the heather hard, but deep are the ditches.'

'Hold him!' shouted Ianto. 'I am coming to shoot.'

The hare ran, and he fired his gun, and the hare was untouched.

'Jawch!' he said. 'Why you did not hold the hare?'

Katrin gave him the insolent eye of the faithless wife.

'Harmless,' she said, 'is a fool's gun.'

But he was away after the hare, and she went to her house.

The weaver spat on his hands and held the plough and spoke gently to the horses, and the hare returned and walked between the heels of the horses and the nose of the plough, guiding the ploughman. In three days the field was ploughed, and champion ploughers declared the furrows were champions among champions.

The weaver sowed and haymaked, and throughout this time Ianto neglected his land and crops to hunt the hare, and were it a man who had stolen his money he would not have hated it more.

The wheat was ripening.

'How did I speech?' he said Katrin. 'Hares and hares. One million hares are eating my corn.'

Each day he walked and creeped and crawled, but each time he shouldered his gun, revenge blinked his eye and shook his hands, and he killed no hare. So concerned he was that he had neither mind nor eye for his wife's fulness.

'Jawch!' he said. 'A witch is the hare and a witch the weaver.

The same day they came and the one is the other.' He shouted: 'Weaver! Where you are? Weaver, come here! My gun is loaded and go you or your ear I will shoot off.'

In common with chance sponers, the weaver was glad to evade his bundle of sin with such ease, and Katrin said no far'well to him.

The corn was ripe.

'My corn-cutter will slaughter the hare and all hares,' said Ianto.

He got the knife of the cutter to polish and sharpen.

'The gleam will spell them,' he said, 'and back-step and back-step they will like walkers sleep and in the last patch they will be rounded and beheaded. But first the head of the hare. Ho-yes, the head of the hare I will bring you.'

'And if you do not bring the head of the hare, will you leave your own in the patch?' said Katrin. 'I need no man on my farm.

Husband and wife heard a thin laugh. The hare was on a hedge, laughing. In his surprise Ianto's whetstone ran along the edge of his knife and blunted it.

The hare laughed again and again.

'Witch hare,' said Ianto, 'tomorrow you will be in my belly.'

'A hare laughs,' said Katrin, 'for a funeral.'

'The funeral of the hare from mouth to belly.'

In the morning Ianto rode round and round his wheatfield on his cutter with his gun at his side, and Katrin tumbled the sheaves from his wake. The sun shone on his frill of hair and made it glisten like a yellow coffin. Round and round he rode and by and by he was on the brim of the last patch.

'Watch you for the death screams,' he said.

The cutter struck a stone.

'Jawch-jawch!' he said. 'This is the witch hare's doing. Ho-ho! I see him. Wo, mares.'

He seized his gun, but before it was at his shoulder the hare had leaped up to him and was clinging to his frill. He screamed and called Katrin to his aid, but she had fallen in labour. The mares bolted, and still the hare did not let go its hold, and his head was drawn down and down, and a wheel caught his frill and the knife slashed his throat.

The hare panted to the moor to bring back its wives and children it had shepherded there for refuge. But they would have nothing to do with a husband and father who had taken them out of corn into a wilderness, and they scratched its nose, bit its ear, and tore its fur. It escaped and hid until it was recovered and then came to the farmhouse.

Katrin, nursing her child, saw it, threw a log at its head and killed it.

# A Widow with a Full Purse Needs No Husband

A pale slight woman aged forty was removed from the post office where she was employed to post office Aberbedw. So on a morning she presented herself to the postmaster in his room.

At the sight of her the postmaster said in English:

'Good morning, madam. Very nice weather and how you are and what can I do for you?'

'I am the new clerk,' she said.

'You are not Welsh naturally,' said the postmaster, and greater praise than that no Welsh person can give another.

'Clear Welsh indeed!' she said in Welsh.

'Here's surprise!' the postmaster said in Welsh, and this was the language they spoke to each other for ever after. 'I thought you were a ladi. Hap you are one in spite of being Welsh. What capel are you?'

'Methodins.'

'I am Congregationals.'

'Ho, then.'

'There is room in my pew.'

'You are obliging.'

'No. I do you a religious service, and perhaps you will do the same for me. Take off your belongings and leave them here.' The postmaster cried at his door, which opened upon the counter: 'Here is the new clerk. Show her about and about.'

He was tall and baldish and his stomach was sunken, and he was a good servant. But now his mind was upon the woman, and for her tidiness and trimness he gave her the endearing name Miss Fach. He compared her with the five other women at the counter: red-cheeked wenches who were two lumps in front and one behind, and their ears had been bitten from leaning on the counter for to hear lewd sayings, whereas she was demure and sedate and as genteel as the English.

During the morning he went to her and took her aside and said to her:

'Welsh men have sweet tongues and loose morals.'

Before he turned to go to his room, Tim pigger came and cast his eyes on the floor to see what he could find. He was the lusty fellow who combed the beach and searched the streets for lost treasure and whose hair reached his shoulders and beard his navel. He lived alone in the same house as his mare and pigs. 'Where do you have pigs to make fat?' one would ask him for his comical answer, this being the answer: 'Replies they are to prayers.' There was no sense in that, because the man never went to capel, and only capel prayers go to Heaven.

He raised his eyes and saw Miss Fach.

'Dammo!' he exclaimed. 'The slimmest rib in a town of fat women. You are a tidy morsel, strangeress.'

The five women laughed, and one said:

'Have her for wife, Tim pigger.'

'Your manners are not official,' was the postmaster's rebuke. 'Pigger, Miss Fach has not one or two things to say to you. Good-bye and poof off.'

Tim fumbled his cap.

'Why for you make a riot, postmishtir, and poof? Your belly bellows are broken, man.'

At that Tim departed, the peak of his cap at the back of his head.

With each day the postmaster's affection for Miss Fach

deepened. He tried to make a portrait of her, and used many sheets of blotting-paper and grades of black-lead and colours of crayon, but he was not satisfied with his work.

He called her into his room.

'Stand there,' he said, 'for a look round you. Your likeness is inside me, but will not flow to my fingers. An angel church window you are.'

'Flatter me you do,' said Miss Fach. 'Young are angels and a woman am I.'

'Whatever your age, very pretty you are. What is the matter with my pencils I know. Can they make hair like daffodils? Can they make a picture of a flesh and blood angel? Man cannot do what took God nine months to make.'

'Ho!' said Miss Fach.

'A fall of the tongue and apologies. How you are getting on?'

'Quite very well.'

'If impudence you have, report in my office and I will do the what for at once.'

'Troubling you that would when there's no trouble to be.'

'Troublers are the rest of the clerks and darkers. But you are my soul's awakener.'

Everyday he spoke to her after that fashion, and in the evenings he strolled with her along streets of capels and shops and high narrow dwelling houses. One evening he strolled with her beyond the harbour towards the path which winds about the mount called Top Town.

'This is house Tim pigger,' he said of the house aside the foot of the path. 'Smelly of pigs it is! Ach y fy! Blow your nose on the ground.'

Tim was inside the half-door of his pigsty, which was part of his house.

'Fair night, Tim pigger,' said the postmaster civilly.

'Woman fach,' said Tim, 'search with a hairpin and no sponer you will find in postmaster.'

'You are a bad scandal, pigger,' said the postmaster.

'More money I have than you,' said Tim, and this is every Welshman's last word to his enemy.

'We go, Miss Fach,' said the postmaster.

They took the steep path.

'After me and catch my coat-tail,' he said.

'I will catch.'

'Look on my back head and not down. At the bottom Avon Bedw gallops to the sea like a frothy stallion. Now, what you think! The pigger rides up in the night on his mare.'

'Perilous is that.'

'Perilous is the way to Hell. If his horse throws him off that is where Bedw will take him unless a fish swallows him first.'

They climbed upward.

'Soon we will be on the plain,' said the postmaster. 'A plain there is on every Calvary.'

They rested on the plain, he sitting like a goose with cold feet.

'Panting am I,' said Miss Fach.

'Say you pant to Heaven's plain with me.'

'Poor am I, and a poor wife is her husband's burden.'

'A wife is no burden when love is thick.'

'Rich you are.'

'I have a post as long as I am in it and a pension after I am not, and what is the use of a pensioneer hoarding cash? Consider the pigger. Cash he has and dirty it is.'

Miss Fach had something to say which she did not say. It was: 'Cash is never dirty.'

'The more cash you have,' the postmaster said, 'the less you have of what you ought. Do you hear a small noise, Miss Fach? It is the clock of my heart ticking love seconds.'

'Hap I hear and hap I do not.'

The postmaster gazed out to sea.

'If your tongue was ten thousand times ten thousand,' he chanted, 'I would lick it and yet be dry.'

Miss Fach rose.

'Blush you my cheeks,' she said.

'The light of day is darkening,' said the postmaster on the way down, 'but the light of my love is a bonfire.'

They came to her lodging, and at the door the postmaster said:

'Loveless is cash, Miss Fach fach.'

So he could worship in her company the postmaster turned Methodist; and no Welshman can do more for a woman than forsake his capel for her capel.

'Wed you I will,' said Miss Fach to him.

'Amen. Amen. AND AMEN,' said he. 'We will climb Heaven's ladder together.'

The saw is that the rungs of Heaven's ladder are afflictions.

Tim visited the post office some time each day, writing on telegram forms, setting his watch by the clock, asking for stamp edge, today buying a halfpenny stamp and tomorrow trying to exchange it for a halfpenny; and whether he was coming in or going out the peak of his cap was set at Miss Fach.

'Tim pigger,' said the postmaster to him, 'why for you are here when you don't buy?'

'Buy I will, man,' said Tim. 'Tell the bargain price of shop-soiled stamps.'

The postmaster put 'No Admittance Except on Business' on the door.

But he was overreached. Tim deposited a shilling in the Savings Bank on each of twenty days, and on each of the following twenty days he withdrew a shilling. Then Miss Fach received a letter from him, sent O.H.M.S., saying: 'A certain Timothy has a very hot hearth and come you this night.'

She went and he showed her his mare and five fattening pigs.

'Wed you me?' he asked.

'Honest am I,' she answered. 'Postmaster is the husband to be.'

'The fat pigs I will sell.'

'Piglings you will have to buy and pig's food, and where is your profit?'

'Over the mount is my profit,' said Tim.

'Men who chase profit never find it. And, Tim bach, poor are the men who bank in Post Office Savings Bank.'

Tim raised his hearthstone and brought up a box.

'Open and count,' he said.

Miss Fach counted nearly four hundred pounds in paper money and gold coins and large and small silver coins and pennies and halfpennies and farthings.

'Comfortable is your hearth,' she said.

In her bed she came to this: if a man alone could gather so much money, how much and more could a man with a wife gather?

In the morning she said to the postmaster:

'If rich I was I would wed you.'

'I have my post and my pension to come.'

'Your pension will perish with you and black will be my widowhood. My husband to be is Tim pigger.'

The postmaster sought Tim and entreated him to give over Miss Fach, and said to his face:

'Mark you me and mark. Wedding you think you are a woman to go to bed with. A mistake you make. She is an angel, and angels are a terrible disappointment in bed.'

Miss Fach married Tim and soon became a slattern. Often Tim rode up the mount in the night and returned at dawn with a pig in one sack and meal or roots and vegetables in another. The meals and roots and vegetables she cooked in a cauldron and stored the mess in a large hogshead, and of it husband and wife and the pigs ate. In the fifth year of her marriage there were twenty-two pigs fattening and the sum under the hearth was over one thousand pounds.

She had ceased going to capel and people walked wide of her. What odds, she consoled herself. After Tim was perished she would sell the pigs and the house, clean herself and go to capel, and the capel never rejects a widow with a full purse.

A Welshman who has an industrious wife grows lazy. So Tim, and combing the beach one noon he came to a lightly clothed woman lying in the sun; and she was the woman the postmaster had married in the belief that love is an ointment that heals the hurts another love has made.

'A slim ribbess you are,' he said to her.

She laughed at him.

'Cut your hair to stuff my sofa!' she said tauntingly.

Tim went away and cut his hair and beard, and he brought the hair to the woman, and she being asleep, he spread it on her breast. Then he took off his clothes and went into the sea, and when he was up to his waist he shouted.

The woman awoke and saw a handsome hulk of an animal.

Each lost an eye to the other, and in the nights they went up the mount on the mare.

The hogshead emptied.

'The pigs want food,' said Miss Fach.

'Am I the pigs' feeder?' said Tim. 'Go and find food.'

She tramped here and there and stole meal and roots and vegetables; 'and this I do,' she said to herself, 'not for him but for my widow term.'

As she wished the death of her husband, so he wished her death.

'Sound there is,' he said to her, 'of a white she ass on the hill over Rheidol. Fetch me the white ass that I can sell her for money.'

He had not heard of such an ass and he commanded her in the hope she would never return from such a quest.

Miss Fach went up the mount and down the valley other side and up the desolate formless hills over Rheidol. On the second day, or maybe the third, of her journey she saw a pure white ass. 'Come to me, little ass,' she said, 'and carry me home.' The ass came to her and carried her so gently that she was ashamed for the trick she was playing, and she said: 'The husband wants to sell you, little ass, but trot you off after you let me down for fear he sees you and ropes you.'

The ass delivered its burden and trotted away, and Miss Fach entered into her house, and her husband was not there; and presently the postmaster cried at her door.

'Tim pigger! Tim pigger!'

'The husband is not here,' she said. 'Why your shoutings, postmaster?'

'Everybody knows and why you do not I do not know,'

said the postmaster, 'that Tim pigger takes the wife on the mare in the nights for to sin on Top Town. Miss Fach, order you him to stop this abomination.'

'What speech you speak, man! In a book is "Easier to shave an eggshell than the evil on a bad man's heart." Sit you down.'

'I wedded your likeness and there is no likeness.'

The man and woman gazed at each other.

'A looser is the wife,' said the postmaster, 'and I will lock my door to her. Come you to my house.'

'Well, I have the husband, and he is not perished.'

'Hist!' said the postmaster. 'The mare is on the path with the sinners after their sinning. Ho, yes, there they are.'

He and Miss Fach looked through the window.

They heard the bray of an ass, and on a sudden the man stopped, turned, and bolted from the path. Tim shouted and the woman shrieked and the mare tossed them, and shouting and shrieking they tumbled down the hillside into Bedw.

'There is the little white ass,' said Miss Fach.

'Where?' asked the postmaster.

'On the path.' She opened the window. 'Far'well, little ass.'

'I see no ass.'

'She is whiter than white.'

'Ho, that white,' said the postmaster. 'Only angels and beasts have eyes to see that white. Well, now, the sinners have rolled to Hell. Shall we wed?'

'Have I not my pigs to feed?' said Miss Fach.

## Horse Hysbys and Oldest Brother

An old woman and her son and his wife live on a mountain in comfort and want for nothing. The old woman is in a caravan. The man and his wife are in a stone house and work a freehold of nearly forty-three fertile acres, and they have a horse to help them. This is the horse Hysbys, which means 'knowing'.

Puah is the old woman and Bensha her son, Bensha for Benjamin. They are comers from the Rodericks, noted porthmen or cattle-dealers in back time, and before they settled on the mountain Puah and Bensha followed their trade and Hysbys took them about in the caravan.

Hysbys was in his prime then. He was as fast as a sunbeam, and his coat was so yellow that if he were in a field of ripe corn on a sunny day you would not know which was corn, which was Hysbys, which was sunlight. His coat lit the most desolate roads on the blackest nights and enabled him to bring his caravan to a sheltered gap where there was a spring of water and good pasture and easy granary doors.

Between the shafts he was boss. He travelled as he willed, trudge, amble, jog-trot, or trot, and he halted the caravan where he willed. A sharp word of command or a smart tug at his rein and he would prance and rear and do savage faces, or fall on the floor and make his legs stiff like a dying horse, or land the caravan in a bog and pretend he could not pull it out.

Stripped of his harness he was mild and gentle for a knowing horse who understood happenings. Bensha combed and brushed him and spoke friendly to him and gave him sugar to eat. But Puah took advantage of his softness. She blamed him when there was no blame to be: the gap he had halted in was too close or too open, and sometimes for nothing she would tell him to stand still while she got a thick stick to beat him with, and though the stick was a thin twig and she hit him ever so lightly he trembled like a gate in a dry wall and wept for the unjust punishment. It was odd that such a knowing horse did not have the sense to know that as he showed off when he was boss of the caravan so Puah showed off when she was bossess of him.

In the mornings Bensha set out after fat cattle. He was mid-high and gaunt and sombrous, and his neck was longer and more screwy than it ought to be because of his habit of sending his large brown eyes over hedges to see what the cattle on the other side were like; and he walked with thumb in armpit and thumb in fork of cowstick, which was as tall as himself. His pocket inside waistcoat was puffed with paper money and a cheque-book, and he could make money noises in each pocket trouser. Women persons said that Puah belonged to the money and soon it would be supper with her and then bed and Oldest Brother would come and snatch her breath away; and this and that woman said to Bensha: 'Let me now vow the vow to you, Bensha cattler. Yiss indeed and nearer tea than dinner are you.'

Each day he drove the cattle he bought to a railway station to be sent to Shrewsbury or Hereford. In the evenings he squatted with his mother at the cookpot outside the caravan and told her what he had bought and the wiles he used, and her long narrow brown face gleamed and from her mouth came 'True-blue Roderick is Bensha, my Benshamin,' the word being Bensha endeared. By and by she would arise and going up the stairs of the caravan to bed say: 'When I am not, Jiw will choose you a Roderickess for to wed'; and he going to his tent would say: 'Jiw choose a Roderickess like you, little mammi.' Jiw is Duw pronounced wrongly and Duw is God.

On a spring evening Hysbys brought the caravan to a worked-out stone quarry; and in the morning Bensha went after cattle according to his custom, and in the evening he said to his mother that he had not bought a beast.

'In what wilderness have you been, Bensha?' Puah asked him.

'Up and down,' he said, 'down and up.'

After he was gone in the morning Puah called Hysbys to her.

'Put your back to the mountain behind quarry,' she said to him, 'and look right on fruitful fields, look left on fruitful fields, look front on fruitful fields. Are there fat beasts, knowing one?'

Hysbys neighed yes to the right and left and in front.

Whereupon Puah paced to and fro on her long legs, and Hysbys saw she was perplexed and in despair and he was sorry he had witnessed against his friend, and he shook his head right and left and in front of him, and neighed no and no and no. Through the day he had no spirit to break into pasture or pull the latch-cord of a nearby granary door. In the evening he lolled about the caravan to hear how much trouble he had caused.

'Say your affairs,' said Puah to her son.

Bensha did not speak.

'Why for your tongue is not walking?'

There was no answer.

'On your right you did go for fat beasts?'

'No-no, mammi.'

'On your left you did go for fat beasts?'

'No-no, mammi.'

'On your front you did go for fat beasts?'

'No-no, mammi.'

Puah got up from her back head and without pronouncing her benediction she went to the caravan. She closed the door and lit her lamp. An hour, two hours passed and she opened the door and stood on the threshold, and a sack hung from her shoulders and another was drawn like a shawl over her head.

'Bensha,' she said.

Bensha came from his tent into the light.

'You one Roderick seek fat beasts on a mountain,' she said. 'Ho-ho!'

Bensha moved out of the light.

'Are you as shamed of your face as the owl? Say you what peril mountain is in your eye.'

Bensha moved into the light.

'A woman –' he began to say.

Puah broke the laughs that are sobs upon what else he said.

'Is she me? But Jiw chose her that my son shall turn my sweet heart bitter. Yiss-yiss and so-so. Take five pounds, six, take the price of a prize bullock to her and "Mammi has none but me" say you. "With no me perish she will and so long, woman." Do this, little seedling that came into my furnace.'

'My mouth and ears the woman is. Me she is.'

'Go to her! Hysbys, morrow we leave for far.' Puah closed the door.

On the morrow Bensha was not in his tent, and the paper money and cheque-book were on his pillow. 'Hysbys, get your harness.' Hysbys gathered his harness, but she did not harness him. 'Bensha will come with noon.' At noon: 'Bensha will come eats cookpot.' At cookpot: 'Hap and for sure a mist is on mountain and Bensha is caught.' She climbed to the roof of the caravan and swung her lantern till daylight.

There was no peace in Puah's breasts. Now they cried vengeance, now wailing was heard in them. She gathered clay and made an image of her son, and she tore hair from her head and planted it, hair by hair, on its head and clothed it with his clothes and put the money and cheque-book in pocket inside waistcoat; and she laid it on his bed in the tent. 'Bad will I spell, good will I spell, bad will I spell. Bad, good, bad. Good, bad, good.' While she was trying to make up her mind with what spell to cast on her son through his image, Hysbys looked into the tent and whinnied, and she knew the likeness was faithful. She breathed at the mouth and spoke at the left ear, ear of the heart. This has brought the dead back to life. 'Forty for the poor bullock.' 'You do not buy my bullock for forty, cattler.' 'Forty my last word.' 'Fifty as I live.' 'Forty my last word.' 'Hard you are, Welsh gipsoon.' So on. The image did not breathe or speak. Oof coorse not.

Puah would go to her people, families of whom lived near cattle-fair towns: Lampeter, Carmarthen; and she would say to them that Bensha had turned his loins from the women of his people and was gone in to an alien and entreat them to let her stay with them. She set westward, saying no word to Hysbys. 'There's slow my pace. Teats of my two breasts show my feet the way.' Her feet carried her to the mountain pass.

'Fair day for you,' a man said to her.

'Fair day for you,' she said. 'Know you a certain Bensha? No thing is he to me.'

'The Bensha is every man to every man,' the man said. 'My cow ate and ate and had no time to chew her cud and was perishing. "Bensha," I did say to the Bensha, "save my cow." Beer of powder epsom and shinshir and seeds anis and gin he poured into her and my cow is healthy and wise.'

Farther on she said to a man:

'Know you a certain Bensha? No thing is he to me.'

'Tidy is the Bensha,' said the man. 'Barren was the ten or nine acres he married and drier than a dead man's veins. He sniffed water and found it. "Very much water have I," he said to us his neighbours. "Make courses to bring water to your places." Rare is the farmer who makes a gift of water.'

Another man said:

'He and the woman his wife are breaking the wilderness and who can tell how much mountain will be their garden before their spin is spun?'

Puah turned and came to the quarry. She placed on the heart of the image a marigold, which is a heart strengthener, and she breathed and spoke as she had done formerly; and this she did for three days, and three days, and three days. 'Jiw-jiw, overlook your daughter who is a iobess. You did spit on the clay. I spit on mouth, eyes, nose, ears, heart. Say you to you they are your spits. You whiffed your breath into Adam and a sinner he was. Will you not whiff a mouth of breath into the bellows of this morsel of clay without sin that I shall have a son for the one I have lost? Waiting am I, Jiw. One, two, three, and off you go. Hysbys! The clay breathes. Kneel you, Hysbys. Kneel you, my knees.'

They two were yet on their knees when through the thick darkness a buxom hefty woman came into the tent and said: 'My husband the Bensha is running on the mountain and Oldest Brother is after him. Have you no trick, Bensha's mammi, to cheat Oldest Brother?'

Hysbys arose and stole away and the women did not take any notice of him because their concern was Bensha, and they gazed into the blackness around them and neither could think of a trick that would cheat Oldest Brother.

'Ghost of sun is speeding down mountain,' said Bensha's wife.

'Hysbys is the speeder,' said Puah, 'and Bensha is on his back. Speed, little Hysbys, speed.'

'Woe me and woe,' said Bensha's wife. 'Oldest Brother is on his tail.'

Hysbys toppled Bensha and then he came to the door of the tent and stopped there, and Oldest Brother leaped into the tent and pounced on the image and snatched its breath away.

## *The Earth Gives All and Takes All*

A tree of wisdom grew inside a certain farmer and sayings and sayings fell from it. The farmer gave hundreds of sayings to his neighbours and the over-freight he stored in his head. The store grew and pushed out his forehead and the back of his head and made them like very big puff-balls. Give thanks his skin was thick and not the heathen's, as thin as the skin of an onion. He was proud yet unhappy: he could not sleep for the babble in his head and he was in a fear it would burst up. So he asked the tree how should he dispose of the over-freight. 'Go far,' said the tree. 'Land have I to till and cows and sheep to tend and a horse to work. Do you tell me to hire a servantess to labour while I go wisdoming?' 'A wife is the best servantess.' 'I will wed me to a hefty young wench.' 'Forty years and also seven you are, and will you wind up the sun for another?' 'Silah schoolen I will wed me to.' 'Woman who makes children school obey her will obey her husband.' Of course, the tree did not speak: its sayings fell into the farmer's mouth.

Silah schoolen was a tidy bundle and she was dressed as if every day was a Sunday. She was not tall or short, fat or thin; her cheek-bones were high and her lips were wide and her top teeth swelled from her mouth in a showy white arch.

The farmer came to the threshold of schoolhouse.

'Hoi-hoi,' he said. 'Stop the learning and come you here.' Silah came to him.

'Hear I do you are for auction,' he said.
'Who is the bidder?' asked Silah, pretending she did not know.
'A farmwr well to do.'
'What is the bid of the farmwr well to do?'
'Forty acres and livestock, dresser and coffer and press and settle and tables and chairs.'
'A man with no bed needs no wife.'
'Forgot I did. A bed there is.'

Silah put her hands on her back and divined. Finger one for no, finger two for iss, finger three for no, finger four for iss, finger five for no, finger six for iss, finger seven for no, finger eight for iss, finger nine for no, finger ten for iss. She did this three times to be sure of the correct answer, and three times is lucky.

'Well-well,' she said.
'I will wed me to you,' said the farmer.
'You the one well to do!' Silah said, pretending much surprise.

He clapped Silah's right hand with his own right hand; and he appointed their wedding-day at the time of the rising of the bees.

'Cold is this piecess of clay now just,' she said, 'but the well-to-do one will warm her.'

He looked at her shoes and, leaving her, said:
'Buy you for you hob-nail boots.'

Silah proclaimed the week before her marriage a holiday and on the day of breaking up she made gifts to her twenty-one scholars, giving each a stick of chalk and a certificate merit.

The farmer was at her door.
'In a big haste am I,' he said.
Haste in a husband to be is a well-known happy omen.
'I am no sampler, little farmwr,' she said.
'My shirt I pull off for you.'
'I turn and close my eyes.' A man's gift of his shirt to a maid is a very warm omen. 'Is your shirt pulled?'
'Iss.'

'Iss your coat on and buttoned?'
'Iss.'
She turned to him and he gave her his shirt, saying:
'Wash you the little shirt for my wedding. Good-bye now.'

She did not bring the farmer any money; and the man who marries nothing ends in nothing. She put two certificates merit on the dresser with pen and ink handy for writing the farmer's name on one and her own on the other; and this would be this week, for sure next. The farmer's thin hay was cut and in common with ladis she went into the hayfield with a rake when it was cried in. There was no corn to cut because the seed had failed, wherefore the farmer lamented and cried out: 'God bach, I did the sowing. You did no growing.'

Silah wore soft shoes and did not work outside the house and the farmer slighted his land and livestock for to carry wisdom to his neighbours and persons who were not his neighbours. He was unlike other farmers on and about Avon Hope in South Cardiganshire. They hold that a man is boss of his wife and with a wife who will not work it is 'One dozen kicks have I in each boot, ladi and madam.' This farmer milked his cows before he went forth in the morning and again in the night however late he returned. Other farmers would repent their marriage, but there is no repentance in a man who carries a heavy crop of wisdom.

The days were shortening and he was not able to say all his sayings between milkings and every night he came back with a bushel or so. He was grieved and shook his tree and this fell into his mouth: Wisdom makes the wisest wiser. The meaning under the word was plain. On the second Tuesday in November, that is the first day of the hiring year, a servant man came to his place.

The man was Ianto, and he was like a pillar of good earth and his eyes were as brown and uncomplaining as those of a willing horse. His hair was thick and white, but the freshness of his earth told his age to be no higher than forty.

'Hard work,' said the farmer to him, 'earns the well done and a parcel of the Better Land.'

Ianto did not make holiday on Christmas after day, or Whit-Monday, or August first Monday, and he did not ask for a drib of his wage; and he never went beyond the hedges of the farmer's land. Towards the end of his year he made up his think to tell the farmer he would not hire himself for another year because he was off to find the parcel of better land. But he let days go by without doing so. His nature was harmless and he knew the farmer would be unwilling to part from such a diligent servant who worked as if every day was a frosty day. It was frosty on the last morning of his year and he was bringing lime into a field with a cart and horse and tipping it into mounds; and while the lime was being tipped the horse wore his coat on its back for warmth, but in going to reload he hung it over his own shoulders. He was very cold within and without and he could not speak directly. He brought his bowler hat over his red ears and put his hands in his pocket trouser and pressed his finger-tips into his flesh through the holes therein.

'Hapus is the labroor whose work is his fire,' the farmer said.

'The day is the day and morrow is morrow,' said Ianto, hoping the farmer would fall upon the hint.

'Simple man bach, today is, tomorrow is not.'

'Hearken you now, little farmwr.'

'Hands are busier when the tongue is still. Hoo-hoo, lime in my pair of two eyes!'

'Off am I on the morrow.'

The farmer filled his long, sombre cheeks with breath, which he poohed in a dismal whoo.

'Off you do go and very quick.' That is what every farmer says to the good servant who leaves him.

The farmer walked towards his house. He shook his tree that he should tell the news to Silah wisely and well for she was full of bitter, but nothing fell. The house was built of mud and rubble and by the Bible in the parlour his people had lived in it for over two hundred years; and if the parlour was small it was sacred as the room where infants were baptized and dead rested. But the kitchen was large and the ceiling hooked for hams and sides of bacon and the table on the flagged floor was big enough to cure a pig on it; and everything was orderly. The floor was clean, the cases of the grandfather clock and the weather glass and the dresser and the yellow wardrobe were bright, the jugs and plates and tureens on the dresser shone, and everything was neatly arrayed on the window sill: boot polish and boot brush, cactus in a pot, two Bibles and two hymn-books of a size convenient to carry to capel, the farmer's razor and shaving brush, which was also a clothes brush, the two certificates with their faces downward.

Silah was tidying her hair at the wardrobe mirror, and she saw the farmer in the mirror.

'Limper you are than a sick man's whistle,' she said to him.

'I did rise from my bed and ate my breakwast and I –'

'Why for you cackle before you crow?'

'The frost froze my nose drops and look you now how they boil and bubble. Ianto is off on the morrow.'

'No matter. Half a man can work this small place and one half and under you are. My tongue is spread with sour lard. Rotting apples fall without shaking the tree and are left on the earth. Work you your land and manure it with your rotting wisdom.'

'Ianto will call for his wage.'

'Call on your wisdom to pay it.'

'He will call on a poor dab with nothing.'

'Work pays debts, not sayings. Why I let my bright scholars school I do not know. Here's disgrace. Ianto goes with no wage will be the spitey clonk. Schoolen wedded her to pockets with holes. More spitey the struth: Schoolen is wedded to an empty ring.'

The farmer lamented in this manner:

'Who is the friend slow to come and quick to leave? Money. Why this ill luck on a slim man brimming with bright sayings?'

'Fertile in sayings, barren in wisdom,' said Silah.

She sobbed.

'Know you of no spell to make Ianto forget his wage?' the farmer asked her.

'Spells there are to forget God, but none to forget money,' said Silah.

Ianto came to his dinner and he was covered with lime and his cap was in the belly of his trouser.

'A bush of blossom May is your hair,' said Silah, and she did not know why she said it.

'A burning lime kiln is his body,' said the farmer.

Silah placed bread and bowls of cawl, being a hotpotch of boiled swedes and cabbage and potatoes and fat bacon, on the table. Ianto blew a wis-wis-wis into his bowl. He blew when he awoke in the morning, at the beginning of every meal, when his horse halted to do a to do. Now he laid his forearms on the table and spread his elbows, and he brought bread and spoon ding-dong to his mouth.

'Satan had spit bad in you,' the farmer said to him.

'Spit you over a wall, Ianto bach, and there you are,' said Silah.

'Boils larger than prize onions grew on the hired man who galloped from farm Gadarine,' the farmer said.

'God will watch over Ianto bach,' said Silah. 'Iss He will stand him up against temptashiwns bacco and dablen and sinemma.' A woman named Emma was the first sin filmess.

'What neighbour wishing me bad did hire you on the sly?' said the farmer.

'Bop-bop,' said Ianto as he said at the end of every meal and day. 'The well done I have won and the better land I go to.' He went about his work.

Silah turned upon her husband and said to him:

'Full of words, full of mischief. That is a byword and true.'

'Chaff is Ianto.'

'Where there is chaff there is corn. Your loft is a nought.'

A saying fell into the farmer's mouth. This: Out of noughts deathless things come.

The light was turning melancholy.

Silah washed the bowls. The farmer walked to and fro. He looked through a bottle-glass window pane.

'The sieve is sifting snow,' he said. 'After snow rain and

chilblains and how can my burning dear feet follow a jogging plough? Woe and woe.'

'A dog barks,' said Silah. 'Hap he is good luck.' She let the dog in. 'A black dog on a snowy day! Sorry luck you bring. Out you! Are you as black as the black tongue of Judas?'

The dog turned from her and put up its tail, the end of which was white; and Silah gasped in wonder and she gave it a bowl of cawl.

'Is your message then that there is a lantern on the tail of the blackest night?' she said.

Ianto was at the door.

'I will now milk,' he said.

The farmer was going to speak.

'Lock your lips and go milking,' Silah said to him.

Who knows why the farmer obeyed her?

'Pull your coat down, Ianto,' she said. 'White snow you are. Wet your shirt. Pull your shirt down. Stand you straight. Feet together. How many whites there are?'

'One white,' said Ianto.

'Poor your schoolin was. White lime, white white snow, white pink flesh of man. Three whites. Say you now where the Better Land is?'

'My nose will smell my own.'

'If your nose roved the sky and iss if it turned the face of the moon to the wall you would not find the Better Land. No indeed. The Better Land is only a Bible promise and Bible promises never become gifts. Stand you now in the cornel and clap your eyes and wish three times and then twelve times like this: "How now a well done and a bit of land?"' While Ianto was wishing Silah wrote well done and his name on a certificate. 'Here is your well done and the command is give Ianto the farmer's parcel and livestock and implements.' She stepped into the parlour. 'I do thanks give the pounds of your wage into collection plate Heaven,' and she turned over leaves of the Bible noisily and counted up to thirty-five. Then she came back to the man.

'Clap hands on the deal,' said Ianto.

'Clap God's hand. Hand up and clap.'
She told the farmer what she had done.
'Without reason is greed,' he said.
'Not for you I did, you mackerel in dry sand, but that voices shall not laugh at me or teeth sneer.'
'Deeper is a woman than her petticoat,' said the farmer.

Ianto wiss-wissed the mornings earlier than any woman in the district. He did not do in daylight what he could do by candlelight; and no bop-bop of day caught him with anything undone.

He sold a litter of piglings and six sheep and he got guano and seeds and dairy cake, and the money he had left he put in a tureen.

The farmer mended his pockets trousers with pins and some of the money went in one pocket and some in the other. There's boastful he was before people. He slapped a pocket with a hand and 'Rich am I,' he cried, and the pin pricked the hand and the money fell out. Thus with the other pocket. No matter, no matter. What other sun there is than wisdom.

Silah remained at home, a ladi in soft shoes and Sunday clothes. She gave to Ianto to eat, but did not eat with him or speak to him: he was only a hired iob and as soon as there was enough money in the house he would be shown the trick that fooled him, paid his wage, and sent away. 'You dirty my floor,' she said to him one day. 'Your food I will bring to you out.' This she did. Very well then and so-so for several days. She did not know why she watched the swing of his body when he scattered manure or hide behind the door of the cow-house to hear him flatter the cows into yielding their milk or stand at her bedroom window on lambing-time nights to follow the light of his lantern. He walked on the earth with his eyes on the earth. For sure and for sure he spoke to the earth with the tongues of his boots. Long before spring reached summer's brim the small fields were lively in their many shades of green and heavy crops were foretold. Silah chided her cloth and she drew the hobnail boots on her feet and hung a sackcloth upon her waist and went to him, saying:

'How you are?'

The man and the woman laboured through the days and long into the nights; and the farmer said of them: 'Poor dabs. The earth is their bride and they the grooms.'

The first year of War Number Two brought more money to the little smallholders and freeholders than they had thought there was in the world, and there was no welcome for the farmer and his sayings anywhere. No matter, no matter. He would store in his loft as many sayings as he could comfortably. The tree withered. No matter, no matter. His store would last him one year two years. Yet he was sad and his heart tumbled about and about in its hole. He looked into his loft and all his sayings were dry dust on the floor. Come, Oldest Brother. Before he was cut down he called Silah to him and said to her: 'Do you now look for me in pulpit Tabernacle King David Proverbs because I will be in hole deaf and dumb. Far'well.'

The earth gives all and takes all, and Silah and Ianto caressed and kneaded the earth and they poured their water upon its backward places.

Silah was tossing sheaves and Ianto was stacking and she picked up two sheaves on her fork.

'A poser for you,' she said. 'What is one and one?'

'The cow will calve this night,' said Ianto.

'The easy answer is one and the farmwr has been dead a respectable year.'

'She will calve before the wiss of day.'

Deep in the night they waited upon the cow. The lantern swung in the cow-house and the door was open that they could see through the window how the cow was doing.

'The wish of a cow is a calf,' said Silah.

'Restless she is,' said Ianto.

Darkness was falling into the pool and light was climbing upward.

Silah chanted as follows:

'Two things are a farmer's delight, a horse who is glad to see him and a piecess of clay to warm.'

'Long is the calf in coming,' said Ianto.

'Thirty gates and nine have I closed behind me,' said Silah, 'but the clock in my breast is at noon.'

'Hard in labour is the cow fach.'

They hastened into the cow-house. The cow calved and they cleaned the calf with hay and put it in a crib.

'Bop-bop the day,' said Ianto.

# Bibliographical Notes

### Short-story Collections by Caradoc Evans

*My People: Stories of the Peasantry of West Wales*. London: Andrew Melrose, 1915; London: Dennis Dobson, 1953 (edited by Gwyn Jones); Bridgend: Seren Books, 1987 (edited by John Harris).
*Capel Sion*. London: Andrew Melrose, 1916.
*My Neighbours*. London: Andrew Melrose, 1919. Published March 1920.
*Pilgrims in a Foreign Land*. London: Andrew Dakers, 1942.
*The Earth Gives All And Takes All*. London: Andrew Dakers, 1946.

### Sources for this Selection

A FATHER IN SION. As 'The Man Who Walked With God' one of 'Two Welsh Studies', *English Review*, April 1915, 25-36. Revised and retitled, the first story of *My People*.
THE WAY OF THE EARTH. Third story of *My People*.
GREATER THAN LOVE. Thirteenth story of *My People*.
BE THIS HER MEMORIAL. One of 'Two Welsh Studies', *English Review*, April 1915, 25-36. Revised, the ninth story of *My People*.
THE TREE OF KNOWLEDGE. Third story of *Capel Sion*.
THE PILLARS OF SION. Fifth story of *Capel Sion*.
THE DELIVERER. Eleventh story of *Capel Sion*.
JUDGES. As 'Judges in Sion', *New Witness*, 23 March 1916, 640-41. Revised, the twelfth story of *Capel Sion*.
THE DAY OF JUDGMENT. *English Review*, February 1917, 127-31. A sequel to 'Judges'.
THE ACTS OF DAN. Fourteenth story of *Capel Sion*.
THE WORD. *English Review*. September 1916, 221-25. Revised, the second story of *Capel Sion*.

THE COMFORTER. Fifteenth story of *Capel Sion*.
AN OFFENDER IN SION. *Everyman*, 21 September 1917, 560-61.
A WIDOW WOMAN. As 'A Widow Woman in Sion', *Westminster Gazette* [*Saturday Westminster*], 2 June 1917, 1-2. Revised, the tenth story of *My Neighbours*.
JOSEPH'S HOUSE. *English Review*, August 1919, 141-47. Revised, the eighth story of *My Neighbours*.
EARTHBRED. *English Review*, March 1918, 227-33. Third story of *My Neighbours*.
ACCORDING TO THE PATTERN. Second story of *My Neighbours*.
FOR BETTER. Fourth story of *My Neighbours*.
SAINT DAVID AND THE PROPHETS. Seventh story of *My Neighbours*.
YOUR SIN WILL FIND YOU OUT. *Wales* 8-9, August 1939, 214-19. Rewritten, the first story of *Pilgrims in a Foreign Land*.
CHANGEABLE AS A WOMAN WITH CHILD. Twelfth story of *Pilgrims in a Foreign Land*.
A WIDOW WITH A FULL PURSE NEEDS NO HUSBAND. Fourteenth story of *Pilgrims in a Foreign Land*.
HORSE HYSBYS AND OLDEST BROTHER. *Welsh Review* 4 (1945) 100-03. As 'Oldest Brother', the third story of *The Earth Gives All And Takes All*. Both texts published posthumously. The sounder *WR* text is here preferred.
THE EARTH GIVES ALL AND TAKES ALL. First story of *The Earth Gives All And Takes All*.